<u>STUFFED</u>

A Thanksgiving Romance by

Jessica Gadziala

"None of this book was written using AI tools. Each word was crafted with human hands."

Stuffed

Callie

      I haven't been home for Thanksgiving in six
years.
      Six.
      It wasn't that I didn't love my family. I did.
They were my everything. It started innocently enough.
My first year in college had been kicking my butt both
with course work and also the fact that my parents were
covering half my tuition, but the other half was mine.
They didn't believe in handouts, but in hard work. So I
had taken a job in an all-night diner right off campus and
because I was the lowest man on the totem pole, I got
stuck working not only Thanksgiving, but the day before
and after. My parents, ever believing being a good,
reliable employee was an important moral to uphold, had
understood and said they would see me the next year. But
the next year was the same drill. The third year had me
laid up with the flu. And my final year had me in a
somewhat nasty car crash that had me in bed with a
concussion and black eye.
      After college, I went to work. And work took
me to Washington, D.C. and too far from Massachusetts
to do the holiday.
      Because when my family did the holiday, they
did it. Meaning it wasn't only the day; it was the day
before, then Thanksgiving itself and the Friday and
Saturday following it. Also, when schedules allowed,

Sunday breakfast as well before everyone hit the road.

I just couldn't swing it.

But seeing as I always made it home for Christmas as well as Mother's and Father's day, they let it slide.

My family was good at not being overbearing.

But, for the first time in six years, I had off. I had a sneaking suspicion that I had off because my company was slowly but surely going under and wanted to cut some corners by cutting some hours under the guise of giving us a long holiday.

See, I had been seeing the signs for months. Which meant I was putting on weight. I mean, not a huge amount. I wasn't at the point where I needed to buy a new wardrobe yet, but my pants were getting tighter. I had just put on some extra padding for the cold season.

This was thanks to the fact that when I got stressed out, I ate potato chips. And when I ate potato chips, I didn't just eat a handful. Oh, no. I attacked the entire bag like a bear preparing for hibernation. Let me tell you, I have become a real connoisseur too. Plain potato were best for a real binge, when you're double fisting the greasy goodness while rocking in your office cubicle trying not to worry about what would happen to you if you found yourself suddenly unemployed. Sour cream and onion was also good for that too. Barbecue and salt and vinegar varieties were good for a little anxious grazing, but not Defcon One level panic because if you ate too many, they made your tongue hurt.

And they had to be chips.

Combos, Fritos, and Bugles need not apply.

I also think it went without saying that baked

and low-fat varieties could take a hike as well.

"I can hear that bag rustling," my mom said, stopping in the middle of explaining the five-day-long event she had planned to do so.

"Keep going," I urged, sneaking my hand in carefully.

"Please tell me you at least got them at Whole Foods."

My mom was a bit of a health freak. I mean, she wasn't ridiculous about it. We would have pies and marshmallows on our sweet potatoes and all that jazz, but they would all be organic ingredients that she paid way too much for at either a local mom-and-pop market or, as she mentioned, the local Whole Foods. My dad was on the same wavelength as she was about food, something that kept them both svelte and active. It also rubbed off on my brother who spent a lot of time in the gym. That being said, he was a firefighter and being active and healthy was an important part of the job.

I was the freak who binge ate chips and had very strong opinions about ice cream flavors.

I did thank the fact that I grew up with her healthy food though, because I think it did some kind of magic to my metabolism that allowed me to binge eat chips for months without gaining more than ten or so pounds.

"I got them at the convenience store on the corner," I admitted, lying to my parents, even as an adult, being a foreign concept to me.

My mother clicked her tongue but kept her opinion to herself. "Anyway, what was I saying?"

"You were just starting to say who was gonna

be there," I reminded her, curling the top of my chip bag and tossing them to the side, making Albus, my very black cat, meow at me and move out of the way. I swear the smug little jerk was sent by my mother to give me disapproving looks every time I ate something I shouldn't.

"Oh, right. Well, myself and your father, of course. Grandpa too. Your cousin Amy will be coming too." I felt my lip curl at that, but said nothing. There was no love between me and Amy, mostly because she didn't give a hoot about family obligation when it came to high school where she and the rest of her popular friends made fun of me whenever they got a chance. I hadn't been the most obvious target, being just a little bookish and just a little shy, with maybe a bad choice in glasses, but I had been an easy target because I had never stood up to them.

"Cory?" I asked, meaning my big brother who I felt like I hadn't seen in forever.

"Of course," she said, sounding a bit distracted all of a sudden. "And he'll be bringing Adam with him as always."

"Adam Gallagher?" I shrieked, not meaning to, but totally unable to keep it in.

My mother paused. "Yes, honey. We don't know any other Adams."

Okay.

Alright.

It was okay.

Sure, I had maybe had a big, giant, life-altering crush on the guy my entire awkward adolescence, but that was a long time ago. I was a grown woman. I had convinced myself I had buried that nonsense along with my maybe a bit too embarrassing pig figurine collection when I had left for college. I had even convinced myself that I barely remembered the guy. And I pretty much had.

Until my mother said his name.

Then it all came crashing back.

The way I used to discreetly watch him, usually from behind one of the books I always had my nose buried in. Quite often while sitting beside the pool while he and Cory swam with friends, wrapped in my cover-up with huge, dark, prescription sunglasses, so no one could tell I was ogling him.

What can I say?

He was gorgeous.

And he was older.

He was eighteen to my fourteen and I knew that even if my breasts were more than a wish and a prayer, he still wouldn't have looked twice at me. You know, being over six feet, muscled, dark-haired, light-green-eyed, chiseled-faced, and charming and all that jazz.

I was just the little sister annoyance he put up with because he was best friends with my brother.

So I watched in all my unrequited hopelessness from afar until, well, I went to college and didn't happen to see him anymore.

I guess it made sense that he would be at Thanksgiving. In his first year of college, his parents had both met with early graves due to a car wreck and a bout with cancer. My family and his had always been really tight and we were all he had left for things like Thanksgiving.

"Callie, hellooooo," my mother called and I realized I had spaced out.

"Sorry, Mom. What was that?"

"I asked when we could be expecting you?"

"Oh, um... well I can leave Wednesday morning. So I should be there by that evening, depending on traffic and how many stops I have to make."

"Honey, fly in," she said, like she always did.

"I have Albus."

"And the airline has a place for pets."

She did have a point. If there was anything I hated more than flying, it was driving long distances. "Alright. I will look at the flights and let you know."

"Okay, honey. Text your father. He will be there to pick you up."

"Alrighty. Need me to bring anything?" I asked, knowing she would tell me no.

"Just your appetite," she said and I smiled. That wouldn't be a problem. Especially seeing as being at my parents' house meant my chip supply would be limited to whatever I could stash in my luggage. Which, well, wouldn't be nearly enough. Especially with the added stress of Adam Gallagher to eat about.

"Can do. I'll see you Wednesday."

"See you Wednesday. Love you."

"Love you too," I said, hanging up, and turning to Albus. "So, we have to have a talk about the travel carrier..." As if he understood me, he gave me a hard look, and ran underneath the couch. "I figured that would be your feeling on the matter."

On that thought, I got off of my couch and moved into my bathroom, closing the door and checking myself out in the full-length mirror attached to it. I pulled off my giant sweater, leaving me in yoga pants and a lightweight tank, my usual bum-around outfit.

"Not that bad," I told myself, turning to the side and putting my hands to my belly. It really wasn't that bad. If I didn't have such unforgiving eyes, it probably wasn't even noticeable. I hadn't been exactly a stunner to begin with, being average in most ways, including my build. I wasn't fat, but not thin or overly curvy in the *right spots* either. I wasn't tall, or short. My hair was long, but a kind of messy mass of wavy medium-golden brown. Nothing exceptional, and it was usually piled at the top of my head in a messy bun. My face was purely my mother, which made me view it more kindly than the rest of me. I had her pale, milky skin, her naturally arched brows, her slightly oversize mouth, her understated nose, and her cheekbones. The only thing I got from my father, aside from my love of books, was his very light gray eyes.

I turned, looking over my shoulder at my butt, then back around to fully face myself.

Not bad.

And maybe if I could cut the chip compulsion out for the next couple days, it could be even more not-bad.

But, really, what were the chances of that?

Especially with the knowledge of Adam Gallagher sitting across the dining room table from me and going to the football game with us and picking late season apples with us.

He would probably be doing it in a three-piece suit, being a big time lawyer and all.

And then an image of Adam, older, probably a hell of a lot more handsome with a little age, something it seemed only men were capable of. *The bastards*. Adam Gallagher with maybe a little stubble on his face that got a little more chiseled with age? Oh, yeah.

I sighed, shaking my head at my reflection.

Yeah, the Adam thoughts were definitely not going to help the anxiety thing.

I moved out of my bathroom into my bedroom that I had a sudden surge of insecurity about. As if he would see me and somehow magically know that my bedroom had seen more *literary* action than physical action in a long time. This was shown in the fact that the right side of my bed was piled with at least six books and the sheets were pink and the comforter had little pink and purple flowers on the cover. I was no nun. I had shared my bed with a man or two. Okay, literally only two. And then there was a boyfriend in college along with one God-awful one-night stand I was still trying to forget. That being said, the last man who warmed my bed was...

"Jesus," I said, stopping dead in my tracks on the way to my closet.

Eleven months.

I hadn't been laid in *eleven* months.

I went into my closet and dragged down the big, rolling purple suitcase my parents had bought me when I went off to college, in hopes that I would return frequently. I had an almost overwhelming urge to rip off the TARDIS patch I had sewn on the week I got it, wanting to give it a little personality.

Like it mattered if Adam thought I was a nerd.

I had always been.

Things like that never changed.

I opened it up and piled in leggings and jeans, some tees, autumnal sweaters, one dress, and pajamas. I paused as I went into my underwear drawer, shaking my head at the selections. Was there anything more telling of (almost) a year of celibacy like a underthings drawer full of beige, white, and black?

On a sigh, I went back into my bathroom to get my sweater, slipped into shoes, grabbed my purse, and went out the door.

To buy new underwear.

And another bag of chips.

Plain potato.

It was a Defcon One kind of night.

Callie

I was trying to ignore the pain on my arm under my sweater from where Albus had scratched me as I walked through the airport, pulling my purple bag behind me, holding Albus' carrier in the other, with a messenger bag full of books (okay, and some chips. Not a lot, I swear) worn cross-body in my funky fall-leaf printed leggings and giant (literally four sizes too big) gray sweater that almost came down to my knees and a pair of knock-around flat-heeled brown boots. My hair was in a messy bun on top of my head and my somewhat big hipster-ish black-rimmed glasses on my nose and pillow marks from my nap on the plane on my cheek.

It was a look.

But my father was never the type of person to notice things like that, being a retired school teacher and current guest professor, far too studious to care about fashion trends. It was perhaps what I loved best about him. And when I stepped outside and found my father waiting for me in a giant brown sweater with elbow patches that he had literally owned (and worn) since I was in elementary school, with his horn-rimmed glasses and sturdy oxfords on his feet with a book tucked under his arm, yeah, he was a real sight for sore eyes.

He gave me a one-armed hug, as was customary

for him, and a kiss to the temple as he reached for my suitcase. We started walking toward the car and he nodded down to my messenger bag. "What'd you bring?"

I felt myself smile, never having found anything more comforting than a fellow bibliophile. "A little Hardy and some new paperbacks I found on the new release table."

"And?" he prompted with a knowing smile.

"Okay so I brought some Austen too. And maybe a collection of Poe. That's it, I swear."

To that, he smiled warmly. "You do remember that I have all of those in the library at home."

"My copies are prettier," I insisted. And they were. I was a sucker for new cover editions of classics. The Austens I had were in vibrant pink and purple and had matching edges to the pages.

He tisk-tisked me as he put my suitcase in the trunk and opened the backseat for me to deposit Albus and his carrier. "Since when have looks ever mattered?" he asked as I got into my seat and shivered a little, waiting for the heat to warm up.

"Oh, since about middle school. But I love that you never saw it that way," I said honestly. "So is Mom in a tizzy already?"

"Your mother?" he asked with a head shake as he turned us into traffic. "You know, I don't believe that woman even knows what a tizzy is."

That was true enough. My mother, for all her perfect micromanaging, was never left scrambling. Everything went to schedule. I guess that was what made her an amazing project manager.

"How's work been, Cal?"

I felt my stomach clench hard at that, not wanting to lie, but also not wanting to worry them over the holiday either. "They recently joined up with another start-up," I said truthfully, leaving out the fact that the new start-up and the owners of said start-up were the reasons the company was going to go belly up in less than a year. The greedy jerks had a good thing going before then. Now everyone was going to be out of a job because they thought they could get bigger and better and richer.

"Seems a little soon for that," my father said, biting on the inside of his cheek, a habit I inherited when I was mulling something over.

"Yeah. Who knows. Let's not talk about work when that's what has kept me away for Thanksgiving for six years."

"Fair enough."

"Did Cory make it in yet?"

"You know your brother," he said with a nod. Meaning, Cory never missed an opportunity for a home-cooked meal, even though he was closer to thirty than twenty.

I nodded and let the silence fall between us, resisting the urge to ask about Adam. Partly because I didn't want to know and partly because I really did want to know and didn't want anyone else to know that I really wanted to know.

We pulled into the drive about an hour later, the sound of some education CD in the radio keeping us companionably occupied.

My parents had a lovely home. Really, even as an adult, I marveled at it. My father, bless him, never had any need for something quite as large and sprawling as their house. And he also never made the kind of money that would afford one. But my mother, for all her drive, did make that kind of money and did want the three-story Colonial in a pretty light green color with crisp white trim. Really, it was two full floors with a dormer, three of those windows sticking out of the brown roof. I had a soft spot for that very top floor where I had insisted they move me when I was ten years old. Each of the windows had a built-in window seat with comfortable cushions so I could sit and read while looking out at the kids in the neighborhood playing. I loved the low ceilings and the way there were nooks and crannies everywhere. My room took up half the floor; the rest was made into a sitting room that my mother occasionally used when she wanted to get away from everyone and get some extra work done.

The land was pretty big, just shy of an acre full of big, old, sturdy trees, including a surplus of weeping willows that I always loved. There was a built-in pool set back from the house with a black fence around it and an assortment of chaise lounges. It would be covered now, I realized with an exhale. It would have been nice to lay by the pool and read.

And maybe see Adam in a swimsuit again.

"Come on, Cal," my father said, making me snap out of my thoughts. I got out, still wearing my messenger bag and going to get Albus as my father disappeared inside with my rolling suitcase.

"Dad where did you..." I started, walking down the hallway with the wide-planked floors and white shiplap walls toward the large rectangular kitchen. The kitchen was one of my favorite rooms, after my old bedroom and father's library. It was pure my mother, upscale but still country chic. The cabinets were a light sage green. The backsplash and countertops were a mix of different browns and tans. There was a giant island in the center and all the appliances were oversize and stainless steel. To the right of the room was what my mother called her "all season room". It was really just a continuation of the kitchen where a white rectangular table was situated in a sun-washed space because the windows went from floor to ceiling.

My mom was facing away from me, her brown hair in a clip at the base of her neck, her thin body clad in black slacks and a simple camel-colored sweater. There were the unmistakable strings of her apron tied into a bow at her lower back. My brother was sitting on the island, picking at something there with his two fingers. Cory got the lion's share of good looks in the family, leaving me with the leftovers. He was taller, leaner, with a strong jaw, a refined type of forehead, my mother's blue eyes, great lashes, a roman nose, and all the fashion sense the family had to offer. He was dressed in dark wash jeans and a light blue button-up that he had tucked in with a brown belt and matching shoes. His brown hair was a little longer than it should have been, but Cory was notoriously bad about remembering to do normal tasks like getting his hair cut.

But my mother and Cory and the smell of cooking food and the nostalgia of being home, yeah, that wasn't what stopped me dead in my tracks.

No.

That would be none other than the towering form of Adam Gallagher standing to the side of the island in black slacks and a gray dress shirt that he tucked in.

There was no tie or jacket and he had the sleeves of the shirt rolled up to his elbows, showing off strong forearms and a very expensive-looking watch.

I'd been right when I said he had probably aged well.

I was also right about how unfair it was, especially given that he was a looker to begin with.

But, as fate would have it, the years were uncommonly kind to him, making his already chiseled face look even more cut, his jawline stronger, his forehead more distinguished, his cheekbones just a little deeper. And his body, yeah, well it had certainly taken on a more masculine form too- all wide shoulders and strong chest under his perfectly tailored clothes.

His light green eyes were on me and the impact of his gaze somehow made my lungs feel crushed and a slight blush rise up in my cheeks.

It didn't exactly escape me that he looked like he stepped out of a mens catalog and that I literally looked half-homeless.

"Callie," he greeted me first. His voice had gotten better with age too, deeper, smoother. Like a fine Scotch. Not that I knew anything about Scotch, but in books, that was how a man's voice was described. And it seemed more than fitting. And it totally made my belly do a weird wobbly thing. "Nice to see you again."

"I, ah, nice to you again too." I felt my eyes go huge at that mumbling idiocy. "See. There was supposed to be a 'see' in there somewhere," I rushed to cover, my sweater suddenly feeling way too hot. I shook my head and swallowed past the strangled feeling grabbing my throat. "How have you been, Adam?"

Albus chose that second to shriek in the carrier, slamming into the side of it and making the whole thing shake in my hand.

"Alby!" Cory said, hopping off the counter and coming toward me.

"Al*bus*," I corrected, as I always had to.

"Stupid name for a cat."

"It's distinguished," I clarified.

"It's the name of some fictional wizard, Cal," he said, smiling in a very big-brother condescending way as he reached for the carrier, set it down, and freed Albus. "God, remember her dragging us to those midnight releases, Adam?" he asked, reminding me yet again that said man was still in the room.

"I'm pretty sure I bought her a wand at one of them."

He totally had. It was *The Half-Blood Prince*. I had been fourteen; he and Cory were eighteen. And because Adam was the only one with a car at the time, our parents had conned them into taking me when it was literally the last place in the world they would have wanted to be on a Saturday night after their high school graduation. But they had taken me, dressed in my freaking Hogwarts robes and more excited than I had ever been for Christmas. And Adam had totally bought me a wand. It was Hermoine's wand and it had meant the whole world to me that summer. And, well, several summers that followed. I still had it sitting on a bookshelf at home.

"Honey, what are you wearing?" my mother finally broke in. I looked over to find her shaking her head at me, but smiling like she expected nothing different.

"Oh, ah, I... didn't think we would have

company just quite yet."

"Really, Pip?" Adam asked, shaking his head like he was offended. "I'm still considered 'company'?"

My heart crushed inside my chest at the nickname that stemmed from the time when I was eight and positively *obsessed* with *Pippi Longstocking* and insisted everyone call me Pippi from then on. In all his twelve-year-old annoyingness, he had continued to call me it even after I begged him to stop. But as I got older and my feelings for him went from a little sister type adoration to something less innocent, I got butterflies every time he said it.

I forced a little smile, trying to keep things light. "I haven't seen you in six years, Adam."

"But here you are," Cory said, either sensing the mood was a little tense or just being his usual carefree self. "Looking like a hipster librarian."

I sighed, taking the hit because he was right.

"Why don't you go put your bag and Albus' carrier in your room?" my mother suggested, giving me an out I very desperately needed.

It took everything in me not to run out of the freaking room.

I was pretty sure I didn't take a breath until I opened the door to my old bedroom, exhaling hard and taking a deep breath, noticing my mother must have put some kind of air freshener in there because where it used to just smell like old paper, it suddenly had a cinnamon spice thing going on. It was a simple room and left mostly as it had been when I left home six years before with my full-size platform bed with a foam mattress I had worked a summer to afford because spring mattresses could never seem comfortable enough for long spans of binge reading. The bedspread was the same worn starburst-style quilt my grandmother had made me before she died, all pink and yellow and purple. The bookshelves were full of my old favorites, but the ones I had grown out of enough to not bring with me when I moved.

I resisted the urge to go over and run my hands over the spines like I used to as I dropped the carrier and tossed the messenger bag onto the bed. I reached for the hem of my giant sweater and hauled it off, leaving me in a black tank top and the leaf leggings.

"Don't change for me, Pip," Adam's voice said from behind me, making my heart fly up to my throat as my stomach dropped to my feet and I let out a small squeak as I turned, clutching the sweater to my chest.

"No. I wasn't. I mean... this was just comfortable plane clothes."

"Liar," he said, giving me a wicked smile as he moved in from the doorway and went over to my bookshelves, running his hands over the spines like I had wanted to do. "I bet that suitcase of yours is full of outfits just like that one."

He wasn't wrong.

"Why haven't you come home in so long?" he asked, sitting down on my bed like it was the most natural thing in the world. It wasn't. Adam, along with any boy or man, was never allowed in my room. Those were the rules from elementary school until I left for college.

"I, ah, was always working."

"Couldn't come just for one day?"

"No."

"Pip..." he said, dragging it out like it had some

kind of meaning. But I had either forgotten how to speak Adam or he wasn't being clear enough.

"What?"

"Never did learn to stand up for yourself, did you? I bet you were the only one stuck at work every single Thanksgiving."

Again, he wasn't wrong.

"Well, I'm here now," I said, trying to keep things light because the way he was looking at me seemed oddly intense and it made me want to discreetly slip back into my sweater and then, maybe, disappear.

"It really is good to see you again," he said, standing. Which was a good thing because I maybe liked the sight of him on that bed a little too much. I had fantasized about just that sight way too many times before I slept at night. Especially after I started smuggling in romance novels to my room in my late teens and got a whole new kind of sexual education. "What's that look for?" he asked and I realized he was suddenly right in front of me, towering over me, watching me with those light green eyes of his.

I was pretty sure my tongue twisted all around itself and got into a genuine knot right then.

I swallowed hard and tried my best to keep his eye contact.

"What look?"

His head cocked to the side, his expression thoughtful. Then he shook his head a little. "Never mind. Your mom wanted me to tell you that dinner will be in an hour," he said, moving away from me and toward the door. "Don't change," he added, back to me, as he went out and closed the door quietly.

I exhaled hard, quickly scrunching up my sweater and putting it back on. I looked over at my messenger bag, thought about the chips, then thought about Adam, and then decided against it.

I didn't go right back down, however, deciding I needed a few minutes to de-frazzle and try to not beat myself up about my less than flattering first re-impression. I had it all planned out. While he was right about my suitcase being mostly full of outfits similar to the one I was wearing, I had also, when I went out to buy new pretty underthings, grabbed a couple decent outfits as well. The type my mother wouldn't be embarrassed to see me in and my father wouldn't even notice. I couldn't change then, after Adam brought it so fully to my attention that I didn't need to change because of him.

But my stupid, over-thinking mind, well, over-thought that.

What did it mean?

Did he mean that he was so used to seeing me look frumpy that he didn't think I could look decent? Or, perhaps, was it the much more innocent idea that because we had practically grown up together, that I should feel comfortable 'being myself' around him?

Either way, I had the sudden, almost uncontrollable urge to go out and buy some makeup, scrounge up my contacts, slip into something slinky, attach spikes to my feet, and prove to him that I could do pretty and that I wasn't, y'know, that silly *Harry Potter* obsessed fourteen-year-old in Hogwarts robes he knew me as.

But that would have to wait for another day, I decided as I went into my closet to look at the mirror attached to the door, straightening my hair a little, then deciding it was time to go back downstairs and be social.

I was halfway down the staircase when I heard my cousin Amy's voice. I immediately stopped, my lip curling in a way that was more habit than anything.

I truly hadn't even seen her face in six years and if I went another six without seeing it after this, that would be just fine with me. There was something about the scars of bullying that never fully went away. This truth was amplified by the fact that one of my bullies was my own family member.

It didn't matter that we weren't kids anymore and it didn't matter that she and her posse couldn't gang up on me and say things that made me want to hide under my covers until high school was over. When I saw her walk into the hall, perfectly flawless as she had been years ago with her effortlessly styled brown hair with golden and honey highlights cut around her very angular, almost catlike face with her big green eyes and her full lips, her thin but curvy body wrapped in casual gray skinny jeans and a tight white sweater, all I could think was: *run*.

But I couldn't do that. There was no dark corner in the library to hide in at lunch time. I had to be a grown up and face her.

I had set my mind to doing that and started down two steps when I saw something that not only made my lip curl, but made my stomach drop.

Amy walked right up to Adam, wrapped her arms around him like they were the oldest of friends.

Then she gave him a kiss right on the lips.

And that was when I oh-so-gracefully missed a step and fell.

Such was my life.

Callie

"Graceful as always, Cal," Amy said, a familiar sneer in her voice.

"You alright, Pip?" Adam asked at almost the same time, but his voice was more amused than concerned. This was likely due to the fact that I had spent my entire childhood and adolescence tripping over anything in my path and often nothing but my own two feet. I rarely ever got hurt. Unless my bruised ego counted. Which it didn't.

"Yep. Fine," I said, grabbing the railing and pulling myself up, only wincing slightly at how much my ass hurt from the fall. "Hey Amy. How have you been?" I asked, genuinely not caring but knowing it was better to show no embarrassment. She would latch on to that and make my day even more disappointing than it already was.

I mean, really, she and Adam were *friendly* like that?

I thought he had better taste than that.

That was ungracious of me, but given how she made my life hell all through high school, I felt justified with a small bit of cattiness.

"Oh, you know me," she said, smiling in a way that was all teeth. Literally and figuratively. "Love my job. Just moved into one of the new townhouses over on

Elm..."

"That's great. Congratulations!" I said, forcing a smile that hurt my face muscles. "I am going to go see if Mom needs any help. I'll let you guys catch up."

"No need for that," Amy said, reaching out and closing her perfectly manicured hand around Adam's bicep. "Adam and I have never lost touch."

Something about the way she said 'touch' made my insides recoil.

Right. Okay then.

"That's great for you," I said, turning and walking back into the kitchen, suddenly all too aware that my own fingernails were definitely not manicured. Actually, they were blunt and had a two-week-old coat of deep blue nail polish.

"Uh-oh. She's got that brow thing going on," Cory said from his position on the island.

"I don't have a *brow thing*. I was coming to see if Mom needed any help."

"Actually, hon, the food is just about ready. Can you grab a couple bottles of wine for the table?" she asked and I went to do just that. I was glad for the distraction because the sound of Amy's husky laughter was mingling with Adam's deep, rumbling kind and it was putting me in a mood. I had no right to feel that way, but I did. I guess spending years curling my lip at all the girls who flirted with Adam was a hard habit to break.

"Here, let me open those," Adam said, coming up behind me unexpectedly and making me stumble into the chair I was standing in front of. He reached out, his hand taking the neck of the bottle, his fingers brushing mine. "I don't know if I trust you with a corkscrew."

I released the bottle, setting the other on the table and moving away from him. I had a feeling that the term 'safe distance' would be applicable to almost every interaction between me and Adam for the length of the holiday. Keeping a safe distance would greatly reduce the chances of me doing something stupid such as blurt out how much I had been in love with him all through my adolescence and that I maybe still wouldn't exactly be adverse to a good roll in the hay with him. Or ten. Or maybe daily for the rest of our lives.

Yeah, because chances were, I would blurt that out.

That kind of thing had *Callie* written all over it.

"I hope it's not too cheesy to be going with an autumnal menu even though it isn't Thanksgiving yet," my mother announced as she and everyone else filed in, most holding bowls or platters. "We have butternut squash soup, a chopped kale, sweet potato, and cranberry salad with a sweet but tangy dressing," she announced putting her bowl down and removing the others from my brother's hand. "Then for the main course, we have stuffing filled baked pumpkins, grilled veggies, and seasoned chicken. Sit, sit," she demanded as everyone moved to stand behind the chairs they intended to take. Which meant Mom and Dad at the ends, my brother beside me, and Amy beside Adam.

We all sat and went through the motions of passing food around. I looked down at my plate, amazed at my mother's ability to throw not one or two, but *six* vegetables into one dinner and it still somehow smelled divine. I owed a veggie filled meal to my poor potato-chip-filled body.

Conversation passed as usual, slightly awkward at first as everyone found their footing, then easily.

Until the inevitable happened.

"Cal, honey," my mother asked, reaching for her wine with her long-boned fingers I had admired as a kid, "how is work?"

My stomach twisted because while I didn't want to, the only way to keep them from worrying was to lie.

"Work is great," I said, false smile in place as I shoved some stuffing in my mouth, hoping they took that as a sign to move on.

"Really?" Amy asked and I felt the food already in my stomach turn sour. I knew what was coming. And, like a train that pulled the brake too late, there was nothing to do but sit back and watch it fly off the track. "I heard that the merger made the investors worry and the stocks plummet."

She said it casually, like we were talking about the stocks for Starbucks, not the company that held my livelihood in their hands. That was Amy though. She had so much practice making people's lives miserable that she perfected the art of blameless backstabbing. But I knew her well enough to see through the careful tone she used. Besides, Amy wasn't in the same kind of business I was. And she damn sure wasn't someone who watched the stock market. So her knowing, it was on purpose. She had looked into me.

And the effect, yeah, it was exactly what she wanted.

My mother's hand froze with her wine halfway to her lips, her whole body getting tense. She, being in business herself, knew how bad that meant things were.

26

When I chanced a look at my father, he looked worried. He never looked worried.

"That's why you finally got to come home," my mother guessed correctly. "They're cutting hours. Have they started doing layoffs yet?"

"Two days ago," I said, deciding honesty was the best route.

"Is your resume up to date? You won't get anything out of them if they just go belly-up. And unemployment will only be eighty percent of..."

"Mom," I cut her off, having caught the look of both interest and concern on Adam's face and not wanting this conversation to continue, "let's not do this now, okay? That's my after-the-holiday problem. Let's not ruin this vacation with work talk."

Cory, ever my champion when he wasn't my big brother tormentor, jumped to my aid. "Yeah, let's move on to politics for a lighter subject," he joked, knowing full well that our parents had a strict 'no religion, no politics' rule for the dining table.

But from there on, the conversation went to lighter things, allowing my stomach to unclench itself so I could eat again. We sat afterward and everyone else had coffee as my mother only served desserts on weekends or holidays, something I both admired and loathed in that moment. I could have used some chocolate.

Because if I wasn't completely mistaken, Amy just kept trying to dig at me.

Why? I had no idea.

Habit, maybe.

Or just her personality.

A bully was always a bully.

And she never could get along with other women, not even the ones in her friend group. There was always some drama or another going on. It was a little sad to be honest.

Men though, that was where she excelled.

Being naturally beautiful and having learned how to dress and do her hair and makeup to further accentuate that fact mixed with her ability to make any man feel like he was the only man in the room, even if she had done the same thing to *every other* man in the room, made her really good at the flirting thing.

And she used all of our coffee clutch to do so with Adam.

By the time my dad dismissed himself to his books, allowing me to excuse myself as well, I was in a mood. I paced my room for a long time. Finding myself too antsy to sit and read like I wanted, I threw on a couple more bulky layers, grabbed my quilt, a book, and a bag of chips and went down the back staircase and into the backyard.

I climbed up into my old tree house, feeling better at just being outside the walls as both Amy and Adam, curled up, ate most of a bag of chips, and read a hundred pages.

I felt infinitely better.

On that note, my tired eyes telling me it was past my bedtime, I climbed back down from the tree then up the back stairs into the loft.

"Pip, where the hell have you been?" Adam's voice asked, a little sleep-rough, making me start and stifle back a scream.

I turned from my focus on my bedroom door to

see him in the living space.

Shirtless.

He was *shirtless*.

And the reason he was shirtless?

Yeah, the pull-out couch was pulled out.

And he had been sleeping on it.

He was sleeping ten feet away from where I would, most definitely now that I knew he was there, *not* be sleeping.

"Callie?" he prompted.

Adam

If there was ever a woman who truly looked like a deer in the headlights, it was Callie right then. Her eyes, already doeishly wide, were even bigger. Her lips parted. Her entire body froze.

No one was surprised when she disappeared after dinner.

It was no secret that Callie and Amy never got along.

It was also a fact of Callie's life that she was completely incapable of facing confrontation. Which was exactly what she would find from her mother if she showed her face again that night.

Sometime around five years old, Pip mastered the art of hiding away. It was her father's doing. Her mother always faced up issues, dealt with them head-on. Her father, however, was much more comfortable letting the chips fall where they may while he went into his library and escaped into other worlds. It was a habit Callie had picked up and amplified as she grew older and learned to read. I'm not sure in the twenty some-odd years that I knew her that I had ever seen her without a book in her hand. Or purse. Or backpack. Or, on the occasion that she wore a sweatshirt, in the hand pocket in the front. It was a truly consistent character trait of hers. She found comfort in written words. When she was nervous and it was inappropriate to actually pick up the book to read it, she could be seen running her fingers over the spines or tracing the designs on the covers.

She carried pens and wrote her favorite quotes on the inside covers.

She collected every possible retelling of her favorites.

She had at least four copies of *Far From The Madding Crowd*. At least. And that was only the intel from the last time she had been home for Thanksgiving to discuss such things with her father.

Six years was a long time.

I think maybe a part of me was worried that the world would wrestle those traits away from her.

Seeing her walk into the kitchen with those leaf leggings and huge, oversized sweater, with her hair in a messy bun and those giant glasses on her face with a messenger bag cross-body that I knew had a load of books in it, yeah, somehow that was almost a relief to me.

Why?

That had a very simple answer that I was trying to ignore.

"What are you doing here?" she blurted out, shaking her head.

I pushed up in the bed, reaching to my side to flick on the light. Her eyes dipped, following my bare chest and stomach to where the sheet bunched around my hips. Her cheeks blushed and her gaze flew back up, not quite making eye contact again.

See, Pip, while good at hiding her true feelings from bullies like her cousin and people who would make her discuss them like her mother, was always painfully transparent to me. So it was abundantly clear that from about twelve or thirteen on, she developed a crush on me. No one else, not even Cory, seemed to pick up on it but me. Or, at least, no one had ever mentioned it to me. And, to her credit, she really did hide it well. But I knew. I always saw right through her.

Six years was a long time and I knew that her childhood crush was buried under other crushes and loves and relationships, a fact that settled a bit like lead in my stomach.

But it was nice to know that there was still a part of her that was attracted to me.

"I'm sleeping here," I said, giving her a lazy smile as she still stood there frozen in the same spot she had been when I first called out to her.

"But... why? You live around here, don't you?"

I did. And it would have been more comfortable to go back to my own house and my own bed where I didn't have a fold-up mattress bar jabbing into my back. But I didn't want to go home.

"Yeah, but you know your mom. She likes having everyone under one roof so she can just call up the stairs when breakfast is done or wake everyone up for midnight hot chocolate." There was enough truth in that for her to believe it, even though I knew it wasn't the only reason.

"But why are you *here*?" she asked, brows drawing together in confusion.

"I'm a little old to bunk with Cory these days."

"Right, but the spare..."

"Amy," I supplied, feeling my lips twitch as I

realized why she was pushing the issue so much. She was uncomfortable with me being so close.

"I don't understand, though. Mom never let any guys up..."

"That was when you were just a girl," I said with a shrug. Her mother's rules were very, very clear about no boys, not even her own brother, being allowed up in her room. "You're all grown up now, Pip."

And she was.

Last I had seen her, she was just shy of eighteen and still a bit waifish, borderline boyish. Or, perhaps it just appeared that way because she was generally in layers or baggy, flowy clothes, forever hiding away. It was something I, fresh from college where girls were often in as little clothes as possible to not offend decency laws, found refreshing.

But when I walked in earlier to her in just a tank top and leggings, yeah, it was clear that the years had been kind to her. Where I remembered her straight up and down, she had rounded out in hip, chest, and ass.

Yeah, she definitely, definitely was all grown up.

And I was finding that that was becoming an issue for me.

"Oh, um," she fumbled, chewing her bottom lip for a second, then shrugging. "Alright. Well, I will, ah, try to keep it down."

To that, my smile broke free.

Aside from a pretty constant issue with remembering how her feet worked and therefore falling on her ass a lot, Callie was one of the quietest people I had ever met.

"You're going to reschedule the wild orgy for another time then?" I asked, chuckling when her cheeks went bright red. When she couldn't seem to come up with anything to say to that, I decided to give her an out. She was tired. It was a long day. And she had an interrogation about her future plans from her mother to look forward to and, if I knew Amy, more not-too-subtle jabs at her confidence. "Go on. Get some sleep, Pip. We have to do the orchard thing in the morning. And your mom likes to get moving early."

She nodded at that, letting out a breath she had been holding since I said the orgy comment. "Right. Goodnight, Adam," she said, turning away and rushing toward her door, closing herself behind it.

"Goodnight, Callie," I called, knowing she was listening.

It was going to be an interesting holiday.

Callie

I was a *grown freaking woman.*

A grown woman who had slept with a man before, who had felt hands on her skin, who had fallen asleep half-smothered by another body.

And yet I found myself awake almost the whole night on my childhood bed, unable to sleep because there was a half-naked man in a bed ten feet and one closed door away from me.

So, alright, it was Adam's half-naked body. That had to be taken into consideration. He wasn't my most recent ex with the pasty-white skin and the charmingly soft belly and spaghetti arms. This was *Adam*. This was the same Adam I had seen shirtless countless times in my life. But the years brought with them the kind of muscles only men could have- etched, deep, the kind of cuts you could sink fingers into. They weren't massive; he was always more of a thin type of strong. But the muscles were even more impressive than I remembered and he had dark chest hair, a trait I was always fond of. Men were supposed to have chest hair. And, well, there was also a small trail of dark hair that disappeared beneath the sheet that took my attention for an embarrassingly long moment.

Then there was that orgy comment, so like him, but still unexpected, and my already activated libido went through the roof. Which left me awake in my childhood bed, trying to suppress images of walking into the other room and climbing into bed with him.

I failed that task until four in the morning came on strong, making my sandpaper eyes insist on sleep. Which I did.

I was startled awake all of two and a half hours later to someone slamming on my door. So accustomed to living alone in an apartment building where I never even bothered to meet my neighbors, yeah, I shot up in bed on a shriek. I was still pushing my hair that had escaped its elastic band out of my face when the door opened and Adam's big form took up my whole doorway.

"Hey Pip," he said, shocking me by moving inside. My eyes dropped and I saw steaming cups in his hands. I was shaking my head before he even said anything. I wasn't a coffee fan. It was something my family both didn't understand and often forgot. "It's tea," he surprised me by saying, moving next to my bed in his perfectly fit jeans and an oatmeal-colored thermal, looking every bit ready for autumnal activities, and putting the steaming cup down on my nightstand.

Then he did the damndest thing.

He sat down next to my hip, looking me over, smiling a bit at my bed messy hair. If I wasn't mistaken, his eyes darkened a little as they dipped lower. My own gaze followed and I realized I had slept in the clothes I wore the night before, sans the sweater and, well, my bra. So I was just in the tank and it was morning-chilly and, as my old college roommate would say, "It was a tit nipply in here for the breast of us". My nipples were sticking out of the material slightly. And Adam was looking.

I wasn't sure how I felt about that.

I mean, on a physical level, I knew how I felt about that. I felt a lot like I wanted to grab his hand, put it over one of said breasts, and see where things went from there.

But it wasn't that simple.

There was history.

There was my brother's friendship to think of.

As well as the relationship between Adam and the rest of my family.

And, not to mention, my poor, battered little unrequited-filled heart to think about.

"You know how many times I have told my mother I hate coffee and she keeps pouring it for me?" I asked, reaching across my body to grab the mug, blocking my breasts from view and his eyes rose accordingly.

"Green tea. Agave, not sugar," he said with a shrug. "Same as it's always been."

Augh.

Of course he remembered that.

Of course he paid attention.

He was one of *those* guys.

The good ones.

The ones every girl dreams of.

Including me.

I took a sip, letting the too-hot water burn my tongue, trying to snap myself out of it. I was just overtired and disoriented. "Is everyone up and dressed already?" I asked as I watched him raise his coffee cup up, black, like always, and took a sip.

"I don't think your mother sleeps," he said, shaking his head, smiling fondly. "She's already elbows deep in egg white omelets."

"Let me guess. Veggies, but no cheese."

He nodded. "With a side of steel-cut oatmeal with fresh berries."

I shook my head, pulling my legs up toward my chest. "Well, on the plus side, I will probably drop a few pounds over this holiday instead of packing them on like most people."

His head tilted, brows drawing together slightly. "You don't need to lose weight."

Okay.

I needed to get the hell away from him.

He was every bit as amazing as I remembered and it was problematic.

"Alright," I said, turning and moving toward the end of the bed, which made my legs brush his in the process. "I better go get ready then before I get blamed for holding everyone up. Is it cold out?"

"Sixty," he said, standing and moving away, giving me the space I desperately needed. "See you downstairs."

With that, he left, leaving the door open because he knew I had to head downstairs to shower. I dug around in my bag and grabbed my small toiletries bag, then took off down the stairs, daringly doing so while drinking tea. Which, for once, did not end up with me burned with it.

I skidded to a halt outside the bathroom as Amy came out, the room a bit steamy behind her. She looked too perfect for such an early hour, her long legs in deep green skinny jeans with brown three-inch booties. She had on a tight brown, green, and white striped fall sweater, her long hair braided down one shoulder. It was an effortless look I knew she put a lot of effort into.

Her eyes dropped to inspect me, landing on my chest, and when she looked at me, she sneered. "A robe might be a good idea when you have men in the house."

Before I could even try to think of something to say to that, she moved past me, brushing into my arm in the process.

I threw myself into the bathroom, taking deep breaths, and curling up my nose to breathe in her perfume. I jacked open the window, much rather being cold than having to smell like her, and stripped for a shower. I got out, brushed my hair, and left it to air dry then reached for my clothes. I realized I had grabbed one of the new bra and pantie sets- white with black lace, and shook my head at myself. Why had I bought fancy underthings again? Some buried hope that maybe Adam would get a chance to see it, perhaps?

Pathetic.

I sighed, getting into the set then dragging on a pair of jeans, a green flowy tank, and an oversized and left-open white cardigan. I slipped into the same knock-around boots as the day before, put on a bit of mascara, and called it a day.

Amy looked over my outfit from her position shoulder-to-shoulder with Adam with a sneer. My mother seemed to give it her approval. My father didn't even notice it.

"Is that an ex-boyfriend's sweater?" Cory asked, reaching for the orange juice. "It's three sizes too big for you."

"Yes, I frequently date men who wear *women's* cardigans, Cor," I said, shaking my head at him.

I didn't look at Adam.

Not once.

First, because I was pretty sure he could see the suppressed desire there. Second, because I didn't want Amy to notice and use that against me somehow. And third, well, my libido had enough to deal with.

"So... apples!" my mother declared as soon as the dishes were in the dishwasher and cleaning.

"Isn't it a little late in the season for apples?" Amy asked in a somewhat condescending tone that had my mother's brow raising.

"Sure is, dear. For Jonathan and Macintosh and all those usual varieties. But our orchard around here plants trees like Keener Seedling, Mattamusket, and Rockingham Reds. They all drop fruit from late September until late November most years."

I pressed my lips together to keep from smiling, loving how my mother was always able to put people in their place without seeming malicious. It was a skill I always wished I could learn. But with a tongue that tended to get all tied up, it was never a possibility for me.

"Alright, so we will take the Explorer with Amy, Cory, and Grandpa," my mother started. "But we don't have..."

"I'll take Callie," Adam said immediately, making me stiffen.

"Or I could go with Adam. We're friends after all," Amy suggested and, for once, I was almost okay with her not minding her own business. Being alone in a car with Adam sounded nerve-racking.

"No, Amy dear, I need you to fill me in about your mother," my mother offered as Adam moved in

40

beside me.

"Ready?"

"I, ah, I just need..." A Xanex. Or Paxil. Or a sudden stomach virus that forced me to stay home.

"You won't need a book, Pip," he said, and I realized he was closer than I thought because his breath was warm on my ear, making my insides shiver a little in reaction. "But I grabbed this out of your father's study just in case," he said, pressing something into my hands. He moved to walk toward the front door as I looked down at the book, smiling a little.

It was an old copy of *Pippi Longstocking* with the green background and two legs up in the air, each with different shoes and different socks on.

"God, I hated that book," Amy said as she passed me, further muddying my view of her.

So then I somewhat reluctantly followed everyone outside, finding Adam waiting beside his late model black BMW, the engine already turned over, heat cranked up to warm it up, no doubt. Him and his stupid thoughtfulness. And he was standing beside the passenger door, opening it up for me as I walked up. I ducked my head and slipped inside as he closed the door, reaching for the radio, finding some oldies station, and cranking it up slightly.

He left it on as he slid in the car and then drove down the side street back toward the highway. But as soon as we hit that long, open road, he reached out and turned it down.

"You know, I once sat and listened to you explain some Shakespearean conspiracy theory, with quoted passages, for about two hours. I swear you didn't stop for breath."

I had totally done that. While, ninety-nine percent of the time, I struggled for conversation, if literature was the topic, I couldn't shut up. "If I remember correctly, it was for your English report in senior year," I said, defending my very long, rambling monologue.

"My point is, Callie, you can talk to me, remember?"

I could.

That was true.

Unlike my brother, he never cut me off when I was rambling or rushed me along while I was stammering or bumbling. He listened. And, what's more, he always seemed interested.

"I don't really have much to say," I said with a shrug. It was true enough.

"We haven't seen each other in six years and you don't have one thing you can tell me about?" he asked and I could feel his eyes on my profile as I looked out the windshield. "I know you spend a lot of time by yourself, with your books, but you have to have something to say."

"What do you want to know?" I asked, never being great with small talk unless someone asked me things directly.

"Where are you living?"

I smiled at that, shaking my head. "A small apartment in an alright neighborhood."

"Where'd you get that cat? I mean, not for nothing, Pip, but he seems to hate you."

The vast majority of the time, that was true.

"He was abandoned by his mother behind my work. His sibling had already died and it was winter and I couldn't leave him out there. I had to chase him for an hour until I could grab him. He scratched me up bad enough to need a couple stitches that night. The vet told me he would settle down eventually. That he was a feral kitten and feral kittens took time, but usually acclimated. And he did in some ways. He knows the sound of the pop top for his food and he's always used his litter box and he doesn't scratch all my stuff up. But he's not my biggest fan."

"He likes Cory. And your father. And he climbed up on me this morning. He likes men."

"Yeah," I agreed, shaking my head.

"Is that because of your boyfriend?"

"I don't have a boyfriend," I said, looking over at him.

"Good to know. Maybe an ex then."

"I doubt it. He hides under the couch on the rare occasion that someone is over. Enough about me," I said, shifting uncomfortably. "How has your life been?"

"Good. Work, mostly. Cory and I go out sometimes. Fixing up my house."

"Fixing up your house?" I interrupted. "Like... with hammers and nails and paint?"

"Yeah, Pip, with hammers and nails and paint," he said, smiling out the windshield.

"Since when are you into home improvement?"

"Since I found a fixer-upper that I wanted to buy. It's been a bumpy road, I'll admit. My old man was handy," he said, shrugging off the memory quickly. "But I never paid that close of attention. And as much as your father has been like a stepfather to me..."

"He wouldn't know an Alan wrench from a

chainsaw?" I suggested, laughing because it was true.

He laughed too, the sound a low, rumbling, warm thing that made my insides go mushy. "You know what an Alan wrench is?"

"I have put together more Ikea furniture than a newlywed couple on a budget. Having an Alan wrench in Ikea and the ability to understand instructions is the equivalent of being a master craftsman."

He chuckled again as we pulled down the long, dirt path that led to the parking lot of the orchard. It was nowhere near as packed as it was during September and October, but there was a smattering of people who were obviously 'in the know' like my mother about apple variations.

Adam parked and we climbed out to be handed reusable shopping bags by my mother who told us to fan out and get as many apples as we could, that she had plans for pies and sauce and who knew what else. So, thankful for the opportunity to go off on my own, I took off toward the rows of trees, weaving in and out until I couldn't even hear my family anymore before starting to look for fruit.

I had about a third of my bag filled when I got the distinct impression I wasn't alone. I hadn't heard anyone, but the hairs on my arms and neck stood up and my belly felt wobbly. I turned slowly, an apple in my hand, to find Adam standing there, his bag already on the ground beside mine, his hands tucked into his pockets, making his shoulders square. His head was ducked to the side, watching me.

"Avoiding me?" he asked, putting me on the spot where he damn well knew I hated to be.

"Don't," I said, shaking my head, ducking to put

the apple in the bag.

"Don't what?" he asked, surprising me as I moved to stand by closing in on me, getting in my personal space. "Don't want to talk to you?" he asked, still advancing, making me go back two feet until the tree stopped me. "Don't be interested in what you have to say? Or, maybe," he said, his hand raising. I felt his fingertips glide over my cheekbone then down my neck as he tucked my hair behind my ear. "Don't give you something you've been thinking about since you were a teenager?" he asked, his hand moving backward to cup the back of my skull.

His eyes got heated.

His head lowered.

And then his lips sealed over mine, seared *into* mine.

Everything, time, space, my heart, my blood in my veins, my body... froze.

I had spent endless hours fantasizing about what it would feel like to kiss him, before I had ever had anything to compare it to. And I was glad for the life experience right then.

Because nothing, nothing had ever compared.

Nothing was even in the same hemisphere.

His hand pulled me closer as his arm snaked around my hips, crushing my chest to his, our bodies molding together, my soft curves to his hard lines. A shiver worked its way through me until my whole body trembled once, making Adam's arms tighten as his lips pressed harder, demanded more from me. Demanded everything. And I gave it. My palms slid over the rough material covering his arms, crossing over his shoulders, my fingertips sifting up into his soft hair. His teeth nipped at my lower lip, dragging a quiet moan from my lips. His tongue slid inside to toy with mine, making me sway against him. A spark of desire shot down to my core, making my sex tighten almost painfully as his tongue retreated and his lips claimed mine again.

A low, needy whimper escaped me and Adam released my lips suddenly, his rough stubble grazing over my cheek as his temple rested against mine, both of us struggling for breath.

My lips tingled, feeling swollen and sensitive.

I pressed my thighs together to try to ease the clawing, demanding need there as Adam's rough breath warmed the side of my face. My own air struggled out of my chest, making my body tremble slightly. His arms closed around me tighter, squeezing me for a long second before releasing me completely.

The air hit my front, warm from Adam's body, somehow shocking the fog out of my brain.

Adam kissed me.

He kissed me.

And it was nothing like I had expected.

It was more.

But, perhaps more so than that, a niggling little thought sprouted, grew, bloomed, until it choked out everything good around it.

Don't give you something you've been thinking about since you were a teenager?

Not only did he know that I had a major, life-altering crush on him as a teen, but he somehow knew that the feelings I thought were long buried could easily be brought to the surface again. Effortlessly, really on his part.

On top of the startling realization that he had known all along the card I thought I kept close to my chest, there was the insecurity in the phrasing he used.

Had he just been doing it because he knew he could? To see if he could get a reaction out of me? To screw with me?

As much as I didn't want to think he was capable of that, I couldn't get over the way he said it.

Why, if it was a genuine moment, wouldn't he say that it was something *he* had been thinking about doing? Why was it on me?

"Adam, where did you run off to.. Oh," Amy said, stopping a yard behind Adam, looking at me. "Has Cal been chewing your ear off about one of her stories or something?" she asked, as my gaze went down to my feet. "Come on, Adam. I found a row full of some apple or other," she said, her voice sweet and persuasive.

When I chanced a look up, their arms were locked as they walked away.

I would like to say it looked like she was dragging him, but it didn't.

Uncertainty, desire, and embarrassment were a heady cocktail, making me feel overheated and itchy and antsy to get the hell out of there. Deciding to trust my flight instinct, I grabbed my bag and followed the path back toward the front of the orchard where I deposited my bag with the cashier, telling her to hold it for my mother, and took off toward the parking lot where I threw myself into my parents' back seat, sinking down and trying not to think.

That was, until my door got wrenched open.

And there was Adam.

Callie

"You're not doing this," he said, shaking his head at me.

"I'm not doing anything," I lied. "I got all the apples they had in my row. I was done."

"And you're in your parents' car instead of mine because..."

"I figured you and Amy would be heading out in the same car."

"You're jealous," he said, smiling like he enjoyed that idea.

"I am n..."

"Yeah, you are," he said, climbing in the back and sitting down next to me, our knees brushing in the small space.

"I don't know if you were aware of it, being so far ahead of us in school, but Amy made my life hell for years," I admitted. "I'm not jealous of her. I just... I know you're a good person and she, well..."

"Callie, I'm not stupid," he said, smiling at me. "She's always been vain and vapid and desperate to have all the attention. But even if I didn't already know that, the way she outed your work issues over dinner last night was all the proof I would need that she's not a good person." He paused and I felt his hand land heavy on my thigh, squeezing. "I didn't know she teased you, Pip. And that sucks. But if she teased you, you have to know it was because she saw you as competition."

A lovely snort escaped me at that as I rolled my eyes. "You saw me in high school, right? Baggy clothes? Glasses? Face buried in a book? I wasn't competition to anyone."

"I saw you, Cal," he said, his arm raising, his finger stroking down the bridge of my nose. "Maybe you were trying to hide away from everyone and everything, but that didn't mean you were invisible. And you were always a threat to Amy and her pretty girl posse."

"You're just saying..."

"I'm saying you are, and have always been, gorgeous. And it's really a shame that you have never been able to see it because everyone else always has."

"Adam, that's sweet," I started, still shaking my head. I would allow "girl next door pretty" if you looked past the glasses and bad fashion sense, but "gorgeous" was a gross exaggeration.

"I saw it," he repeated again, ducking his head a little to catch my eyes. "I noticed. But you were too young, Pip."

My heart seemed to freeze in my chest, a tight, crushing sensation as my belly did a flip-flop that was, at once, thrilling and scary. Was he saying what I thought he was saying?

"Adam, what..."

"I'm saying I was eighteen and you were fourteen and it was wrong for me to even think it. But I thought it."

"Thought what?" I pressed, needing to hear the

words. It was the only thing that could jumpstart my heart again.

"I thought you were the prettiest girl I had ever seen. And, more than that, you were interesting. You know how rare that is to find in someone four years younger than you... at those ages? You blew all the other girls out of the water, Cal. But I was too old for you." His smile went sweet as his hand left my hip, tracing the neckline of my tank top. "Breathe," he reminded me, and I took a breath, feeling my insides get shaky. "So are you going to admit it or not?"

"Admit what?" I asked, looking in those light green eyes of his and completely amazed that they had ever seen me as gorgeous.

"Admit that you had a crazy crush on me as a teenager." My head went to duck, embarrassed for my former self, but his fingers reached out to snag my chin. "Nope. No hiding," he said, pulling my head back up.

"I had a crazy crush on you as a teenager," I admitted, my stomach in knots for some silly reason. He already knew. It wasn't like it was news.

"And that you were totally wondering what I looked like under that sheet last night."

I felt my eyes bug as my cheeks heated. Caught. I was so caught. "Adam..."

"Admit that and I will admit something too."

That seemed like a fair trade. And, well, my curiosity was killing me. "I was wondering what you looked like under the sheet last night."

To that, his eyes heated slightly and he leaned in close, his lips by my ear. "And I have been wondering for years what is under all these thick layers." His nose whispered up the side of my ear. "And what you would sound like moaning my name while I eat that sweet pussy of yours. Or what you would feel like, body under mine, cock deep inside you, while..."

"There you are!" my mother's voice cut in, making Adam pull away while I tried really hard to ignore the pounding of my heart and the almost painful tightening of my sex. "What are you doing back there?" she asked, popping the trunk and hauling the apples inside.

"My car must have been locked so Cal came to sit here. Come on," he said, reaching for my arm to pull me toward the door.

And that was precisely when Amy moved into the doorway. "That's silly. She's there now. Let her drive home with her parents. I will hitch a ride with you."

Really, what could be said?

There was no way for Adam to deny her.

So he turned back to me, giving me a look that I swore said 'this isn't over', and climbed out to go back toward his car.

I took a small amount of comfort in the fact that he bleeped the locks, but didn't open her door for her. That was a bit small and petty of me, but I liked that he didn't give her the same treatment he gave me.

"What's with that look, Cal?" Cory asked, hopping in the back row with me.

"What look?" I asked, trying to instantaneously lose said look that had to be a mix of awe, shock, desire, and disappointment.

The rest of the day was filled with choices.

The choices were which slightly uncomfortable conversation did I want to have- the work discussion with my mother... or the 'we have the hots for each other' discussion with Adam.

I chose the former and offered to help my mother make pies for the next day, knowing she, being an amazing multi-tasking project manager, could likely handle not only the baking but all the cooking the next day by herself, but figuring she would like the chance to catch up with me.

Several hours and a very long discussion about my future later, I went in to sit with my father and discuss books, a bit *too* aware of the sound of Cory and Adam in the other room.

I went up to bed around nine which was entirely too early for me, but it had been a long day and I knew my mother would be up and cooking around five in the morning and I wanted to be able to get up and help her.

I woke up to a finger tracing down the bridge of my nose. Still mostly asleep, I wrinkled up my nose at the sensation only to be shocked fully awake by a low, deep, male chuckle.

"Easy," Adam's voice, quieter than usual, said, his hand landing on my arm and holding me down from shooting up in bed. "It's me."

I blinked into the darkness, my heart a frantic beat in my chest from, at first, being startled awake then, increasingly, the realization that Adam was in my bed.

"What are you doing?" I whispered, trying to squint to see better in the darkness.

"So, this avoiding me thing," he said, his fingers

sliding along my jaw, "is it something I have to look forward to every day until your vacation is over?"

Vacation.

That word made my heart seize.

Because it was accurate.

I was on vacation.

This wasn't my life.

My life was in D.C.

Adam's life was in Massachusetts.

Even if we did finally give in, even if I got what I had wanted for an embarrassing number of years, it would only be temporary.

I would have him for the holiday and I would lose him after.

Suddenly, my heart stopped seizing and seemed to crumble.

"I was kidding, Pip," he said, misinterpreting my darker mood. "I get that you're the type who needs to think things over."

Yeah, things.

Like the possible repercussions of a fling with the crush of a lifetime.

But also at the same time, the regret of not indulging in the opportunity.

"This is probably a bad idea," I said, shaking my head at my ceiling, trying to ignore the way his whole front was near my side, his head sharing the same pillow as me.

"Oh yeah? 'Cause I am pretty sure it's the best damn idea I have ever had," he said, his palm gliding over my shoulder, down my arm, then stopping at my hip, digging in and pulling me until I had no choice but to roll onto my side facing him.

I closed my eyes, pulling in enough air to make my chest hurt before slowly releasing it. It was what I had always wanted, what I had dreamed of. But it was only half. And half of everything suddenly felt like a whole lot of not enough.

"I care about you, Adam," I said, going for rational. "My family cares about you. If we do this, there's a chance things could get weird."

"I care about your family and you too, Cal. I wouldn't suggest it if I didn't think that whatever comes of this will be worth it. Haven't you ever done anything just because it feels right?" he asked, fingers starting to trace shapes into the small sliver of skin between my tee and yoga pants.

"Have we met?" I asked, trying to lighten the mood, trying to put a wedge where I didn't truly want there to be one. "I only do things after long, drawn-out, careful consideration of all possible outcomes."

"Mmm," he murmured, face dipping, his breath warm on my neck. Then, out of nowhere, his hand left my hip and pressed hard between my thighs, making my entire body jolt at the unexpected contact. "Know what the *only* outcome of this," he said, sliding his fingers up to find my clit, "would be?" he asked, starting to circle it carefully as his scruff scraped across the delicate skin of my neck deliciously. "An orgasm," he said, lips pressing into the skin just under my ear as his finger kept up its expert teasing.

My hand slammed into his hard chest, curling in, grabbing the material of his shirt, as a low, throaty sound escaped my lips.

"That sounds a fuck of a lot better than what I had imagined," he said, nipping into my earlobe. His hand pulled away suddenly, making me let out a whimper. "Shh," he told me quietly. "Just making it better," he promised as his fingers slid upward. "Roll onto your back," he demanded and I rolled without even being conscious of telling my body to do so.

Adam pushed up, sitting back on his heels and reaching out for my hips. He snagged the material of my pants and grabbed it, yanking downward. My hips pushed up off the mattress so he could slide the material off my butt and down my thighs. When he freed both my feet, he scooted into the space between my legs, his fingers gently stroking up my thighs, making the skin goosebump in response. My legs fell open as his fingers met my sensitive inner thighs. Then his hands shifted inward, one finger tracing over the lace of my panties, making me suddenly really thankful that I had not only gone out to buy them, but put them on that morning.

His entire body moved forward and down. Before I could even understand his intention, I felt the heat of his mouth close over my sex over my panties, making my hips jerk upward, my legs closing around the sides of his head as my air rushed out of me loudly. The scrape of his teeth moved over my clit, making me moan as my hand slammed down on the back of his head, my hips rising up toward his teasing mouth shamelessly.

His fingers grabbed the material of the panties and yanked them to the side.

I shivered as his tongue traced up my slick cleft slowly, making my back arch off the bed and my head fall back as I struggled to breathe. His tongue found my clit, circling it with perfect pressure as my hand curled into his soft hair, grabbing hard.

One of the fingers holding my panties moved downward, pulsing against the opening to my body for a long moment before languidly sliding inside, making my walls tighten around it, desperate for release.

His finger started thrusting lazily, hinting at what I really wanted and only making me more desperate for it as his tongue kept working me.

My whimpers became low moans as he drove me upward.

Then I lost his mouth as he lifted up and moved over me, his hand flattening over my cleft so his palm pressed into my clit as his finger curled inside me, stroking over my G-spot.

His head dipped and his lips pressed into mine, his tongue moving into my mouth and I tasted my own desire there, feeling my sex tighten at the intimacy of that. Adam made a growling noise in his chest in response, moving back up.

"I've been thinking about this for a long time. I want to watch you come for me."

Then, like my body had been waiting for him to say just those words, a slow, deep pulsation started deep, making my entire body tighten as the waves of pleasure moved through me, his name on my lips as his eyes watched me, heated, and if I wasn't mistaken, satisfied.

As the last pulsations moved through me, he leaned down, planting a chaste kiss on my lips. "I think right then, aside from when you are talking about books, is the only time I have ever seen you completely open. I've got to say, Pip, it's a fucking sight to see."

His finger stayed inside me, his hand in my panties, as he shifted to my side, his arm sliding under my body, his face moving into my neck.

And it was perfect.

It was so perfect that it was terrifying.

Because I had the irrational, bone-deep feeling like nothing else, no moment with anyone else, would ever compare.

It wouldn't even come close.

"Why are you tensing up?" he asked as I finally lost his finger. His hand slid out of my panties and settled over the material covering a sliver of my hip. I shook my head, turning on my side toward him, closing my eyes tight, trying to hold onto the moment while simultaneously attempting to slowly put some guards back up.

Neither was working.

The moment was slipping.

And I never felt quite so raw, so vulnerable before.

"Come on, Cal," he pressed, his voice a little more impatient than usual.

"What do you want from me, Adam?" I asked, closing my eyes tight for a second so they could adjust completely to the dark and I could see his light green eyes searing into mine, reading me, seeing the things I was trying desperately to hide.

I had known men intimately before. I had felt their hands in my panties, inside me. I had known the touch of men I swear I loved. Albeit, it wasn't crazy, uncontrollable, overwhelming love. But it was slowly earned, comfortable love. I had men who I loved that loved me, touch me.

And it had never felt like it felt when Adam touched me.

I couldn't let him see that.

It was irrational, crazy.

Adam sighed, the air he exhaled making my hair brush back slightly and I closed my eyes tighter against his frustration. It was a feeling I knew too well.

"Alright," he said after a long minute, his fingers squeezing my hip. "It's late. We're tired. This isn't the time. Try to get some sleep, Cal. Your mom will be up in about three and a half hours."

With that, his hand left my hip, sliding up my back and tightening, pulling me toward him as he moved onto his back, situating me on his chest.

"Relax," he said, his other hand moving into my hair, stroking through the strands gently as I focused on trying to loosen up.

And while I thought there was no way such a thing was possible, post-orgasm contentedness and fingers stroking gently through my hair, I slowly drifted off to sleep in Adam's arms.

I woke up in the same position a few hours later, on my belly with my leg cocked up high. But my arms were wrapped around my pillow, not Adam.

Because he was gone. I pushed up, disoriented, taking a long minute to decide if what happened actually happened or not. But it happened.

A thousand small things moving through my head, I stumbled out of bed, grabbing clothes, and going toward the door. I could already hear my mother in the kitchen below. I needed to catch up.

I froze as soon as I stepped out of my bedroom though.

Because I had thought that Adam had gotten up early to help my mother.

But he was passed out on the pull-out, shirt off, laying on his stomach, his arm under the pillow, the sheets pooled around his waist.

He had gotten out of bed with me and gone to sleep alone.

I took a slow, deep breath, that hitched a little embarrassingly as I fought back the realization that while I slept, he likely thought. And whatever he thought made him slide out from under me and leave my bed for one he could have alone.

He was putting distance between us.

And I tried like hell to convince myself that that was for the best as I went downstairs to shower and cook with my mother.

But all the while, there felt like there was a shooting pain in my chest.

Callie

Thanksgiving dinner was a huge affair in my mother's house. I had consumed Chinese food or frozen pizza for the previous six years, so it was almost startling to see all the effort and the outcome of all the hard work.

Our dining room took on a harvest theme. The table held a giant cornucopia stuffed and overflowing with deep red apples, green, orange, and yellow gourds, ears of colorful corn, pears, grapes, and leaves my mother had made Cory, Adam, and I collect when we were kids that she glazed and kept as decorations. Two deep brown lit candles sat inside big glass jars on either side of the centerpieces. Bottles of wine, wine glasses, burnt orange plates, bowls, and serving dishes completed the perfectly autumnal look.

Then the food poured in, piling up on the platters on the table and, when that was too full, onto the side board.

It was more food than I had honestly seen my mother ever make, causing me to wonder if she went above and beyond to make sure it was special for me, which gave me a warm, melty feeling inside, giving me a small break from the stabbing feeling that had been there all day.

There were mashed potatoes, mashed sweet potatoes, green bean casserole, corn, cranberry sauce, butternut squash risotto, creamed kale, honey roasted cauliflower, rolls, and cornbread. The giant turkey big enough to feed a small army went without saying.

"Adam, you're next to Callie," my mother said oddly as we all moved into the seats we had used the previous two evenings, me with Cory across from Adam and Amy. The only change being my grandfather shared the head of the table with my father.

"But..." Amy started to object, a little too decked out in a tight flesh-colored long-sleeved bodycon dress with three rows of gold necklaces, and four-inch heels. While my mother liked us to dress for Thanksgiving, she herself in tan slacks and an attractive mauve sweater, she didn't need us to look like we were on the way to the country club to meet our rich, one-foot-in-the-ground husband for drinks.

Adam and Cory were each in slacks with button-ups; Cory's was dark blue; Adam's was a deep green that made his eyes pop all the more.

"We're shaking things up tonight," my mother cut her off.

My head was ducked so all I saw was Adam's torso as he moved away from the seat across from me, rounded the table, and came to stand beside me.

"Alright, sit. Let's have grace so we can eat while everything is hot."

My mother should have been flustered. Her hair should have been a mess. Her eyes should have been puffy and tired. She should have been dragging on her feet.

But, always being the kind of woman I admired, the kind that thrived on activity and a small amount of chaos, she looked instead like someone who woke up at noon, took two hours to get herself together, then met her family for dinner at a restaurant that someone else slaved over for hours.

We all sat, bowed our heads, and listened to my father shoot off a short prayer of Thanksgiving, never being the type who was overly comfortable with religion though I knew he believed.

Then there was chaos as plates were moved around, as wine was poured, as people got up to peruse the side bar.

I had been the last up, letting everyone else fight for floorspace before I went to fetch my own food. When I sat back down, I felt Adam's hand land on my knee underneath the table, so unexpected that I actually dropped my fork, wincing when it clattered down onto the edge of my plate.

"Can dress her up, but can't take her anywhere," Amy said with a smile she thought was light and teasing, but I found menacing.

I had dressed up, though.

Gone was my usual uniform of leggings or jeans and various heavy layers.

I had somehow found the courage to squeeze my slightly wider than it used to be ass into a wine-red skirt with a simple, slightly snug, white v-neck sweater. And ballet flats. Because, well, let's face it, me in heels was just asking for a broken ankle.

So when Adam's hand was on my knee... it was rubbing the silky thigh-high stocking I had rolled up my legs, the smooth friction of his hand on the material making me have to suppress a shiver.

My gaze slipped to my mother as I picked up my fork, noticing the way her eyes almost seemed like they were dancing, and not quite sure what to make of that.

I reached my other hand under the table, grabbing Adam's hand and trying to move it, but he just squeezed tighter.

It stayed there until he needed his other hand to cut up food and the second he let me go, my brain seemed to remember that I was supposed to be eating.

So I set my mind to that and tried really hard to not think about what it meant that he went down on me early that morning, then left me to sleep alone, then suddenly had his hands on me at the dining room table.

Because, really, I would drive myself crazy with that kind of thing.

Dinner was followed with some quick cleaning on my, my mother, and Amy's part, letting everyone's food coma pass. Then the guys were changing for the next tradition- Thanksgiving football.

When we had been younger, it had been all the dads and sons in the neighborhood at the open soccer field behind the middle school. But now that the years had passed, it seemed like it was only going to be Cory, Adam, and all their old friends and fellow ex-football team members.

My mother loaned me one of her expensive cream-colored peacoats because what I had packed wouldn't work with my dressier than usual outfit. Then we were all piling into cars, clutching thermoses of coffee and hot chocolate, on the way to the field.

I was situated on the bleachers beside my

mother. My father was off by the sidelines talking to some of the other older men who had showed up. Amy was, well, being Amy- flirting with all the guys in their long-sleeve tees and basketball pants, touching their hair, squeezing their biceps, letting each of them know that she was on the prowl.

"Alright, spill," my mother demanded oddly.

I turned my head to find her staring at the field as the men greeted each other. "Spill?" I asked, brows drawing together.

"Honey," she said, turning to me with a warm smile. "You spent six or so years completely infatuated with that boy," she started and I felt my eyes bug. So not only had Adam known, but my mother had as well? And here I had thought that I had done a good job of hiding it. "Yes, dear, I knew. You looked at that boy like you had a sweet tooth and he held the keys to the candy store. It was sweet, really."

"It didn't feel sweet," I admitted, surprising myself. But I suddenly felt the need to unload. It was something I had kept so close to my chest for so long; it felt good to share. "It felt like torture."

"Unrequited love usually does," she agreed with a nod. "So then you come back here, six years later, and you look at him just the same as you always did. Then he kisses you in an apple orchard, climbs in the backseat to try to drag you out with him, and puts his hand on your knee at dinner..."

"How did you know about the apple orchard?" I demanded, more than slightly embarrassed that my mother had caught me mid-makeout.

"Honey, I was just walking past," she said,

smiling big, eyes warm. "Looks like he kisses until your toes tingle."

I smiled. "He does," I agreed.

"So, I reiterate my opening statement. Spill."

"I don't know what to spill," I said with a shrug. "I thought it would be different. Six years is practically a lifetime when it comes to things like crushes."

"If you thought that what you felt for that boy all those years was as simple as a crush, you need to re-read those Austen and Bronte books of yours. You loved him, Callie. Rightfully so. He was always so sweet to you."

He had been.

He brought me to midnight releases and bought me wands. He let me babble on about Shakespeare. He bought me a limited edition collection of *The Lord Of The Rings* series. He bought me a ticket to *V For Vendetta* because it was R-rated, but I wanted to see it so badly. He listened when I talked. He hardly ever made fun of me. And even though it didn't add to his cred as a hot, popular athlete to do so, he let me tag along when they went to the movies, bowling, the skating rink, or the mall. And he didn't make me feel unwelcome even though I always suspected I had been, at least a little bit.

My mom was right.

I had loved him.

Maybe, without my realizing, I had never truly stopped.

"You know, I always suspected..." she trailed off, watching the field where the men had moved to huddle.

"Suspected what?"

"That maybe he didn't see you quite as a little sister. But you were so much younger than him. I always wondered what would happen when you two reconnected as you got older. But then you never were able to be back here at the same time."

I felt my lips tip up as I looked over at her. "That's why you put him up by me on the pull-out, isn't it?"

"Can you blame a mom for trying?"

I followed her gaze to the field where Adam was throwing his head back and laughing. We were too far to hear, but I knew that sound so well, I could recognize it in a crowd. "Why bother, though? Our lives are in different places."

She exhaled a little and gave me her full attention. "As someone with slightly more life experience than you, can I let you in on a little secret? It's not the things that we did impulsively, without thought, without consideration of consequences that we end up regretting. It's the things we didn't do, the chances we didn't take, the men we didn't kiss, the love we didn't give. I don't want you to live to regret never knowing what it was like to kiss someone you have loved since you were a little girl. I know you, Cal. You're a perfect mix of your father and me. You, like me, think things through, think them to absolute death more often than not. And, like your father, you tend to hide away from things, live through the worlds other people have created. You would have let an entire lifetime go by and never know what it felt like to really let yourself have something you have always wanted. I figured if I could maybe give a nudge..."

"So you're telling me to let it happen, even if all

I get is this holiday weekend?"

"I'm not telling you anything, Cal. I am just suggesting you perhaps stop listening to your head for a couple of days."

We fell into a companionable silence for a long time, watching the guys play. My mother saw a couple friends and climbed down to talk to them. Cold from sitting still for so long, I got up and walked down the bleachers toward the field as well, resisting a lip curl when Amy moved closer toward me.

"Callie, is that you?" a male voice called, making me jump and turn to see one of the players walking up. He was as good-looking as the rest of them, tall, broad, classically attractive chiseled features, with blue eyes and dirty blond hair. He was vaguely familiar to me. I remember seeing him hanging out with Cory and Adam time to time.

"Hey Matt," I said, giving him a small smile.

"Look at you!" he said, giving me a charming smile, waving a hand at me. "All grown up. You look great, sweetheart."

I felt a slight blush creep up, unaccustomed to being complimented and maybe still harboring the high school girl feeling of "OMG, the football player just said I looked good!"

"Thanks. You look good too."

"How have you..." he started, obviously in full-flirt mode and I wasn't unaffected.

But then I suddenly felt an arm wrap around my lower back as lips pressed a kiss to my temple.

"Hey Pip, cold?" he asked because at his touch, I shivered slightly.

"I, ah, um..." I bumbled, watching Matt who nodded his head, understanding the possessive gesture. "A little," I admitted.

"Don't worry," he said, giving my hip a squeeze, "I'll warm you up later," he said and I felt my stomach drop as he released me. "Ready, Matt?" he asked.

I watched in stunned silence as the two of them ran back off to the field.

I only got about half a minute of shock, though, before I felt a body move in beside me. I didn't need to look to know it was Amy.

"It's sweet of Matt to come over and say hi. I'm shocked he even remembers you."

But if she teased you, you have to know it was because she saw you as competition.

Maybe there was some truth in that after all.

It was no secret that Amy had made her rounds not only on the football team, but baseball and soccer as well. Chances were, she and Matt had had a thing. And, despite her best efforts earlier, he had moved out of arms reach so she couldn't paw at him.

"You know, we're not in high school anymore, Amy," I said, shaking my head a little. "They're not the jocks anymore. And I'm not the nerd." *And you're not the pretty popular girl either.*

She seemed to pick up on the silent message, her eyes narrowing at me.

"And Adam with his sweet big brother act," she went on. "Cute."

I felt my spine stiffen, my mind and tongue seeming to come together in agreement that it was time to stop mumbling and bumbling and pretending her words didn't bother me. For the first time in my life, I was able to stand my ground.

"Hmm," I said, looking at the field. "I'm not so sure about that. I'm pretty sure big brothers don't kiss you in apple orchards or climb into your bed at night and go down on you," I said, moving my gaze over to her, thrilling a little at her wide eyes and open lips. "This cattiness is getting kind of old, Amy. We're not in high school anymore." With that, sure that if I kept talking, I would likely start tripping over my own words and thereby ruin the strength of my argument, I walked off to join my parents and catch up with their old friends.

After football, we all piled in for dessert.

Then Cory and Adam took turns showering off the dirt and sweat from their game.

And, all stuffed and exhausted, we all filed off to bed.

I was woken up a couple hours later to Adam standing in my doorway.

"Pip, come here for a minute," he demanded before disappearing back into his part of the dormer.

I sat up in bed, suddenly very aware that I had changed into pajama pants with bananas printed on them and a giant Hogwarts sweatshirt, but deciding it was too late to change, and moved into the doorway, a little nervous that maybe he was going to expect me to sleep with him.

But when I moved into the room, I found the pull-out couch folded up. Which, well, was weird because since he folded it out the first night, he had always just left it open. It was silly to keep opening and closing it when we didn't need the floorspace. Maybe he had folded it up because he knew I would see it that way and wanted to ease my mind.

"Come on," he said, sitting down on the couch and reaching for one of the giant, soft, knitted blankets my mother kept on the backs of all the chairs in the house. This one was my favorite, a big white and red one that reminded me of Christmas.

"What are you doing?" I asked, crossing my arms, suddenly very aware that I didn't have a bra on.

"*We*," he corrected, "are watching a movie."

"Oh," I said, looking over to see the TV cabinet open.

Movie nights were a big thing when we were younger. My mother used to insist Cory invite his friends over to our house where they were allowed to take over the living room and watch movies and eat junk food and mess around. She figured it was a good way to ensure that they got a little bit of independence while being subtly watched.

I, however, was banned.

By my brother.

"Come on," he repeated, blanket draped down his legs and folded over for him to pull over me when I sat.

I moved across the floor, sitting down as far as I could while still getting under the blanket. "What are we watching?"

"Remember movie nights?" he asked, as if he had read my mind.

"I remember not being allowed to participate," I admitted, curling my legs up into my chest.

"And I remember you throwing an absolute

shit-fit about that Joss Whedon movie."

"*Serenity,*" I said, recalling that night vividly. I, unlike Cory, had been a hardcore *Firefly* fan and had been waiting to see the movie since I heard it was being created. But when he came home with the only copy in town and insisted he and his friends were watching it and I could watch it after, I blew my lid. "I was so mad about that."

"I tried to talk him into letting you in. You with your Nathan Fillion crush."

"Still didn't work."

"It was about ten against one, Pip."

"I bawled my eyes out that night," I recalled, shaking my head at my teenage dramatics.

Adam winced at that. "Yeah, I know. Your eyes were all puffy when I gave it to you when we finished."

He reached for the remote and hit the play button for the DVD player and the opening screen to *Serenity* played.

"I can't believe you remembered that," I said, shaking my head, feeling my heart do the expanding thing in my chest.

He gave me a small smile as he reached over, putting an arm behind my back, and pulled me across the couch until my whole side was against him, my legs pressed up to his stomach. "What part of 'come here' was so hard to understand?" he asked, shaking his head at me as he hit play.

So then we watched a movie that had meaning to both of us.

And all the while, his arm held me to him. His other hand stroked up my arm, through my hair, traced

shapes on my thigh.
It was chaste, sweet, perfect.
And I fell asleep as the credits rolled.
Then when I woke up again, I was in my bed.
Alone.
Again.

Callie

So by the time I dragged myself out of bed the next morning, then all through my shower, and then all through wrapping myself up in full-on defeated black leggings and my old bright orange college sweatshirt that I bought in a men's three-X so it hung down almost to my knees and hinted at no body shape beneath the thick, forgiving fabric, I over-thought, I fretted, I drove myself half-crazy.

My hair went up in a messy bun and my giant glasses went on my nose.

Because I was in a very f-it mood.

"Hey honey, sleep well?" my mother asked, having keen eyes and knowing my f-it attire when she saw it, but saying nothing because both Amy and my grandfather were sitting at the table drinking coffee.

"Yeah. Sorry," I said, shaking my head, knowing she generally wasn't a fan of her kids being lazy. But, well, I was an adult. She didn't get to dictate my sleep and waking schedule anymore. "I was beat from all the cooking yesterday."

"Well, good news for all of us today then," she said, giving me a smile as I made myself tea. "Amy is going to be cooking us dinner tonight. Her mom's lasagna recipe with homemade garlic bread too."

"Sounds great," I said, actually meaning it. I was pretty sure there was some rule in the universe that said when women were in crummy moods, they wanted pasta.

"Yep. Well, on that note, I really should be hitting the grocery store," she said, standing and heading toward the front door at almost the same second that Adam and Cory walked in from out back.

"Actually, I was wondering if you and Adam would be willing to bring Grandpa home for a couple hours?" my mother asked, nothing subtle about it and, judging by the way Adam smiled, he had her number too. "He said he wanted to change out some of his clothes and do some cleaning before he comes back for dinner."

"Sure thing, Pops," Adam said, resting his hand on my grandfather's shoulder for a moment before walking past. "Whenever Cal is ready," he added, doing a quick once-over and when he was done, his lips were twitching a bit.

"I just need my shoes," I said, turning and walking toward the front door where I left them. When I walked back into the kitchen, Adam and my grandfather were in their jackets and Adam was holding out a thermos to me.

"Your tea," he told me and I had to ignore the warm feeling in my chest at the consideration of that.

Did he have to be so good all the time?

"Thanks," I said, carefully taking it so our fingers didn't brush. "Ready, Poppy?" I asked and he gave me a weak smile. He had never been much a fan of family gatherings and I bet my mother's demanding holiday schedule was wearing on him. I wouldn't be surprised if, after we dropped him off, he called my mother to fake some kind of ailment to get out of coming back. The anti-social gene ran strong in my father's family.

"All set," he agreed and we all shuffled out to the car, Poppy going into the front seat with Adam and me in the back, for which I was thankful. "Nice seeing you, Callie-bear," my grandfather said as he climbed out of the car, further validating my belief that I wouldn't be seeing him again until Christmas.

"Climb up, Cal," Adam demanded while we watched him disappear inside his retirement facility.

"I'm good. It's a short ride back."

"Climb up, Cal," he said, half-turning to look at me, his voice a little firmer than usual.

I sighed, not wanting to have a stupid fight over it, grabbed the door, got out, and got back into the front seat.

"Where are you going?" I asked when he turned off the highway that my parents' side street was off of.

"Quick stop, Pip. Relax. No need to jump out of your skin."

He was right; I was anxious. With no good reason really.

I took a deep breath and relaxed against the seat.

That was until Adam rolled his car into the driveway of a somewhat beat-up, okay... really beat-up, three-story, Queen Anne-style home with a dream-worthy wrap-around porch, multi-gabled roof with a domed turret, chipping white and green paint, and old, cracked windows.

"Oh my God," I gasped, shaking my head.

No way.

No way did he live in my absolute dream house.

"Come on in, Pip. I'll give you a tour. Fair warning, it's a mess."

"I don't care if I fall through the floor," I said, already halfway out my door. "What colors are you going to paint it?" I asked as we walked up the front path.

"I was thinking gray with white trimmings," he said, unlocking the front door and opening the door for me to walk into.

I walked right into an impressive foyer, a giant, grand staircase landing leading up to the next floor, openings to the library on the right and the living room on the left with a hall beside the stairs that led to, I imagined, the kitchen and dining rooms.

"Oh, come on!" I groaned, looking over at him. "This is all the original wood!"

He was giving me a big smile, his perfect teeth on full display, his eyes dancing, like he was enjoying my enthusiasm. "Possibly its best feature," he agreed with a nod. "Well, that or the library," he said, holding an arm out to the room in question.

I was shaking my head at him. "Nope. No. I might die of depression at the very sight of it," I said, moving toward the staircase and running my hand over the banister.

"Alright, we can go in there on the way out. Let's head up," he said, moving beside me. "You need to see the master bathroom."

I did.

I needed to see it.

I needed to see every damn inch of the place

and then, possibly, handcuff myself to the bookshelves in the library and never leave.

We didn't make it to the master bath, though.

Adam led me right inside the master bedroom, the only room I had seen so far that had been fully restored. The floors were shining as was the wood trimmings. The walls were painted a cream color that I thought would be better replaced with some kind of patterned white wallpaper, but it looked nice enough. The space was dominated by a giant four-poster bed, stained the same color as all the trimmings and covered in a seersucker cream comforter.

"Wow," I said, shaking my head, already picturing myself sitting on the window seats and reading, looking out on a rain or snowstorm. Like I always wanted. Like I always knew I wouldn't be able to.

Adam's hands slid across my sides, then folded over my belly tight, his warm body moving in behind me, his face dipping into my neck. "You like?" I shook my head. "No?" he asked, sounding surprised.

"I love it," I countered. Then, uncomfortable with the moment, moved on. "You've done a really good job so far."

"Lot of work and I'm pretty sure I'm not sticking to the right style..."

"Wallpaper, not paint," I agreed immediately and his warm chuckle moved through his body and vibrated through mine. Intimate. Way, way too intimate.

His face turned slightly, planting a kiss to my neck, making me shiver. "See? What would I do without you, Cal? Screw up my restoration, it seems," he added as his fingers slid lower, down my hips, then thighs, looking for the obnoxiously low hemline of my shirt and inching it up from where it fell almost to my knees. "Should have come visited you in college," he murmured, making my stomach clench.

"Why?" I asked, my voice a throaty, airy imitation of itself.

"Thought about it a dozen or so times while you were there. Passed by D.C. on a business trip once. Should have popped in."

"Why?" I asked again as his fingers moved the material up my belly.

"You were old enough," he said, his fingers touching the underwire of my bra, exposing the skin to the air as the shirt gathered up under my arms, waiting for me to raise them to free it. And, without thinking, they rose, and he pulled the material off me. His fingers traced across my clavicle then between my breasts, then the center of my stomach.

"Why didn't you?" I asked, my voice wavering as his fingers moved across the waistband of my pants, dipping slightly inside.

"Figured it was pointless. You were all grown up. You must have had the guys in your school all over you. Forgot all about me." I swallowed hard, inwardly acknowledging that, eventually, yes, I had moved on. I had dated. I had lost my virginity. I had loved men. But I had never forgotten him. "Thought we missed our shot. Timing is everything in stuff like this," he went on, his nose tracing up my jaw until I felt his tongue trace my earlobe. "But then you walked into that kitchen, all grown up but the same damn Callie I knew all my life. And you looked at me. And I knew."

"You knew what?" I asked, feeling like I was swallowing past my tongue as his hands started to move down the material of my pants.

"I knew you hadn't forgotten me. Maybe I became background noise, but I was always there. You never got over me." There was truth in that, as uncomfortable as it was to realize, so I remained silent as my pants became loose around the knees and fell to the floor. I stepped out immediately, leaving me in a purple and black striped bra and pantie set. "Say something, Callie."

I shook my head, resting it backward on his shoulder, burying my face into his neck and breathing in. "I don't have anything to say."

He made some kind of noise- raw, primal, making my sex clench tight. "Then let's stop talking," he suggested, his hands moving over my hipbones, then up my belly to cup my breasts over my bra, squeezing slightly.

I let out a small whimper, exhaling my air as his fingers squeezed, making my breasts get heavy with desire, my nipples harden.

"Yeah?" his voice sought permission and I felt my chest warm again. Good. He was so good.

"Yeah," I agreed, leaning my chin up to plant a kiss on his neck.

"Turn around," he demanded as his hands released my breasts, his hands moving to my hips as I turned to face him, my hands sliding up his stomach and chest, finding the buttons of his shirt and slowly unfastening them.

Once the last one was freed, his hands slid from

my hips to my ass, sinking in, and pulling me tight against him, making his hardness press low into my belly, causing a rush of wet to meet my panties, as my forehead met the skin of his chest, taking a slow, deep breath to try to ease the desire that was more like need coursing through my system. My hands reached up, grabbing the material near his shoulders and pushing it off. His hands stayed still, trapping the shirt for a long minute. When they moved away, they pulled my panties down as they went. His shirt hit the floor. My panties followed.

His forefinger moved up my spine, making my head fall back, our eyes meeting for the first time. His other hand rose, cupping my jaw. "That's a good look on you, Callie," he said, his thumb stroking over my parted lips. "Even better knowing I put it there," he said before his head ducked and his lips sealed over mine.

I whimpered into his mouth as his tongue slid forward to claim mine. His fingers worked the clasps to my bra, freeing them. His hand moved from my jaw and they both went to my shoulders, grabbing my straps, and pushing them down. I arched backward slightly so the material could fall. His arms folded across my back, pulling my body flush to his. I moaned as my hardened nipples met his warm skin, his chest hair tickling the sensitive flesh. He made a low, growling sound in response as his tongue retreated and his lips claimed mine again, harder, hungrier.

Then he was moving forward across the floor, moving me backward until my legs met the foot of his bed. His hands moved down to my hips, pushing until I sat at the edge of the bed, making our lips lose each other. When my heavy-lidded eyes opened, I found his equally heavy, needy.

My hands moved up his thighs then across his lower stomach, marveling at the way the muscles tensed under my fingers as I traced down the small line of dark hair that disappeared into his pants. My fingers went to his button and zip, freeing them, then grabbing the material and dragging it down, finding out something I never knew about Adam before. And I had thought I knew just about everything.

Adam wasn't a boxers man.

Or a briefs man.

Or even a boxer briefs man.

Adam went commando.

I heard my air suck in as his cock came into view- hard, straining, thick, and more perfect than I had imagined.

My hands slid up his thighs as I leaned forward, wanting more than I had ever wanted such a thing before, to taste the desire slick on the head. My tongue moved over the hard, but impossibly smooth skin as Adam's breath hissed out of him, his hand landing on the back of my head as my lips closed around him and took him inside my mouth, sucking hard, taking him as deep as I could, feeling my sex clench at the idea of him moving inside me.

"Fuck," he growled as I worked him slowly, wanting to catalog every groan, exhale, inhale, the feel of his hand curling in my hair, the way his cock got even harder in my mouth as I worked him. "Okay, enough," he said, both amused and turned on as his hand grabbed my hair and pulled me backward by it.

I looked up at him, smiling slightly as his hands

reached up to the top of my head, freeing what was left of my bun to let my hair loose around my shoulders. He reached for my glasses next, knowing I didn't need them for close-up, and tossing them in the direction of the nightstand. They missed, clattering carelessly to the floor. I could not have cared less as his knees pressed into the mattress on either side of my body, his arm moving across my back and lifting me, scooting me back toward the center of the bed as he climbed on as well.

I moved onto my back as his body lowered down. But not on top of me. His arms planted by my knees and I felt his lips press a kiss on the inside of my left ankle, then slowly move a path upward, over my calf, the inside of my knee, my thigh, then in.

I moaned loudly as his lips closed unexpectedly around my clit, sucking hard for a long moment before releasing me so he could continue to kiss up the center of my stomach then between my breasts where he paused for a second before his mouth closed over my nipple. His tongue worked over the hardened bud, making my back arch off the mattress as my arms went around him, my fingers digging into the skin of his back. His teeth bit in next, making me let out a half-cry, half-moan at the pain-pleasure mix. His head moved across my chest and gave my other nipple the same sweet torment as my thighs tightened around the sides of his hips, needing more than I had ever needed anything to feel him inside me.

Desire was to the point of pain before I finally felt his body press down onto mine.

His head ducked, his eyes closed tight for a long moment as he took a deep breath. His eyes opened slowly, hazy, as heavy as my own felt. "Perfect," he murmured as his weight shifted to one arm, the other reaching into the nightstand and retrieving a condom, then making short work of protecting us before moving down on me again.

His hips shifted to the side slightly and I felt his cock press against my cleft, the head pressing down into my clit and I sighed out the realization that he was right.

It was perfect.

His lips claimed mine for a second as his hips shifted again and I felt his cock press into my opening.

"I want to watch," he said when I grumbled at the loss of his kiss.

Then, with that, he pressed slowly inside me, so slowly that I felt each inch spread me, fill me, until he was fully inside, my walls tightening around him as my legs folded across his lower back.

And as I looked up into his eyes with him inside me like I had dreamed about for years, that warm, swelling feeling in my chest spread until there was no denying what it was anymore.

Love.

I was still in love with him.

"Fucking years," he murmured as he started to slowly, so slowly, rock in and out of me. "Thinking about this," he added. "Nothing came close to the reality."

Too overwhelmed with both need and emotion, I couldn't find the words to tell him I felt the same way, I pulled him down toward me and claimed his lips as his thrusts got a little faster, a little harder.

My body, long untouched and never more present than right then, drove upward fast, until every inch of my body was tense, poised for the climax.

Adam pushed up, again wanting to watch.

"Let go, Pip," he said, his voice a deep, low sound that shivered through me. "I have you," he said and with that, I shattered. The orgasm moved through my core, a fast, frantic, deep throbbing, that moved outward until it felt like it overtook my whole system.

"*Adam*," I cried when my breath came back.

He rocked into me deep, his body tensing, growling out my name as he came with me.

His body went down on mine after, his head buried in my neck, his warm breath on my skin, making me shiver as I held onto him tight, slight aftershocks coursing through me.

I felt tears sting at the backs of my eyes and blinked them back frantically, not wanting to allow that show of vulnerability. I was exposed enough.

He pushed up a long time later, his eyes a little awestruck as he looked over my face. His hand moved out to trace down my cheek for a second before he leaned down, kissing me slow and deep as he gently slid out of me.

Then I lost him completely as he moved off the bed and toward the bathroom, half-closing the door.

My body, weighted from the orgasm, fought me as I got off the bed, fetched my panties and sweatshirt and slid them on before quickly scurrying back to the bed.

Adam came out a long couple of minutes later, still beautifully, perfectly stark naked. His head cocked to the side, a smile tugging at his lips, as he looked me over. He made no move for his clothes and he came back toward me, climbing up on the bed, moving onto his side, and pulling me onto mine, his arms pulling me tight against him.

We said nothing.

Me, because there was nothing I could say.

You didn't tell a man who you hadn't seen in six years, directly after having sex for the first time, that you realized you were still hopelessly in love with him. With an emphasis on the *hopeless*.

I might not have been an expert on men, but I knew that pesky 'l' word was one surefire way to make a man jump out of your bed like you set his chest hair ablaze.

I had no idea how long we stayed like that.

Time seemed to stand still and slow down and speed up all at once, disorienting me as Adam's fingers moved over me, touching me everywhere, like he was trying to memorize every inch, like he was trying to find each tickle spot and each hot spot, like he had all the time in the world to learn all the secrets my body had to offer.

But then, some indeterminate time later, Adam's phone let out a shrill ring. We both completely ignored it as it went to voicemail. But then it started up again, making Adam let out a grumble as he released me, rolled off the bed, and went in search for his pants that he dragged up his legs as he answered, blocking half of his amazing body from view. I moved my attention to the muscles of his abdomen and chest then, lazily contended, dreamily happy to soak up every inch of a lover's body.

"Hey, Amy."

Her name was like the blare of a alarm clock waking you out of a perfect dream.

I started, my head snapping up to find him watching me, like he had been watching me watch him. He gave me a ghost of a smile as he listened to whatever

Amy said.

"Yeah. Alright. Yeah, Amy. Got it," he said, his voice a bit more impatient, more sharp than it usually was, like whatever she was saying was wearing on his nerves. "I said alright, Amy. We'll be back in ten."

I felt disappointment like a full-body wound as I climbed out of the bed, accepting that our little moment was gone, knowing down to my bones that we would never really get it again.

I slipped on my pants and put my bra on under my sweatshirt in complete silence.

Adam got into his shirt and shoes and grabbed my glasses, also in silence.

There was nothing to say.

As we walked toward the front door, my eyes went toward the library, feeling the sting of tears again and ducking my head as I walked onto the porch, not wanting him to see.

Nothing was said as we drove back to my parents'.

And nothing was said during dinner.

And nothing was said as we all went to bed.

He didn't wake me up.

And he didn't climb in with me at any point.

Because, fact of the matter was, my flight was leaving late the next morning.

What we had was done.

There was no use dragging it out, making it more painful than it had to be.

I was both incredibly grateful for and bone-achingly pained by that.

Callie

A finger traced down my nose, snapping me fully awake the second it touched between my brows, knowing that sensation anywhere as if I woke up to it every night of my life.

"Adam?" I asked, blinking the sleep out of my eyes.

"It's six," he told me, explaining why I still felt exhausted, his hand stroking my hair behind my ear. "You have to leave in two hours," he reminded me, and I felt my heart start to shrink down in my chest.

"I know," I agreed, taking a slow, deep breath.

"I could let you go back to sleep," he said, his hand sliding down my side, his fingertips tracing the side of my breast, making them immediately feel heavy, my nipples hardening in anticipation of more. "Or," he went on, his fingers moving across my belly then down my thigh, sneaking in at the knee and going upward.

"Or?" I prompted, my voice already breathy.

My body, apparently, wasn't overly concerned about the the impending heartbreak, though, because every inch of me felt poised for his touch.

"Or I can take about an hour and a half of that and give you..." he mused for a moment, "three or four solid orgasms and you can catch up on sleep on the flight.

Up to you," he said, dipping his head and kissing up my neck.

Really, there was no choice.

Even though my brain knew it was smarter to leave the memory of us in his bedroom in his perfect house, to let it be a clean break, I knew there was no way I was going to push him away.

"I think I'll go with option two," I said, letting out a laugh/shriek hybrid as his hands grabbed my waist and rolled so he was on his back and I was fully on his chest.

"Smart girl," he said as I pushed up, looking down at him, not even trying to hold back the smile I felt. His hands reached up, pushing my hair behind my ears, smiling back.

"I did graduate top of my class," I laughed.

"And if I recall correctly, you refused to be valedictorian because you didn't want to give a speech."

"Mom was so ticked," I recalled.

"I should have been here for your graduation," he said, eyes a little sad. "You were there for all my things. From graduation to awards ceremonies to all my games."

"You were doing an internship," I said, shrugging.

"Shitty excuse."

"But a valid one," I countered. "I missed six Thanksgiving dinners for work."

"True," he said as his hands slid down and grabbed my ass, slapping it hard once. "Just think, this could have happened six years ago."

I was pretty sure my heart was just a speck of

dust in my chest right about then.

Because what if that was true?

What if I had lost six years because of some stupid work obligation? For, at first, temporary, stepping stone jobs. And, now, because of some company that didn't value its employees enough to make smart decisions and keep them employed.

"Hey," he said, brows drawing together. "Don't do that," he said, his finger pressing into the lines between my brows. "I don't like regret on your face, Pip," he said, his tone so earnest that I had to close my eyes for a second to hold it together. "You know what I like a hell of a lot more there?" he asked, tone going deliberately lighter.

"What?" I asked, swallowing back the last of my emotions and giving him what I hoped was a flirtatious smile.

"This," he said as his hand slipped down my ass and pressed between my thighs. "Yeah, much better," he said as I let out a low whimper, his finger brushing over my clit twice before pulling away completely. When I grumbled, his hands moved out to grab my knees, pulling them up and planting them beside his hips as he folded up, leaving me straddling his waist.

He didn't tease. He didn't make a show of it.

We were beyond that.

His hand snagged the hem of my shirt and dragged it up and off me, tossing it to the floor beside my bed.

His hands planted on my ribs on either side, the tips of his fingers brushing the sensitive undersides of my breasts. My nipples tightened, hardened in response.

"You're so sensitive," he said, leaning forward

and biting my shoulder slightly, making me laugh as my hips dropped down. A gasp escaped me as his cock pressed against me, hard, straining, just a thin pair of pajama pants to hold it back.

His hands shifted upward, cupping my breasts, his thumbs and forefingers rolling my nipples until my hips started grinding down against him, trying to get some relief from the clawing need inside. "Lift up," he instructed, hands sliding down my sides and snagging the material of my pants and panties.

I lifted my hips and he slid the material down, letting me work each leg out, leaving me naked above him.

His hand moved inward and one finger slid inside me quickly, making my walls tighten around him with need. He thrust lazily for a minute, driving me up, before I lost his finger.

He reached toward my nightstand where a condom was sitting and quickly pulled out his cock and protected us.

"Take me in, honey," he said, his voice low and needy.

I put a hand on his shoulder and slowly lowered myself down onto him, feeling him fill me inch by inch. His eyes were on mine the whole time, getting smaller as he slid deeper. His hand moved up, touching the side of my face as I gently started moving against him, too needy to drag it out.

He lowered himself flat on the mattress, his hands resting on my hips, my hands resting on his arms.

"Ride me, Callie," he demanded and I realized I had been still, looking down at him, trying to memorize the look on his face when he was buried inside me.

With that, I started moving my hips, feeling him slide in and out of me, driving me upward fast. It wasn't long before the need for release overwhelmed my urge to keep it slow and sweet and passionate, before I was riding him hard and fast, my head thrown back, my teeth biting hard into my lower lip to keep from crying out.

"Fuck, baby," he growled as I planted my arms beside his chest, moving down over him, burying my face in his neck, my lips pressed into his skin as my whimpers built to moans, trying to stifle them.

His hips started thrusting up into me as I kept riding him, pushing me up harder, faster, until I felt my walls tightening to the point of it almost being painful.

"Come for me," Adam demanded, thrusting harder up into me, one hand on my hip, the other at the back of my skull. "Come," he demanded again as his cock slammed impossibly deep, making me crash hard, crying out his name into his neck as my body shook through the powerful orgasm.

He never stopped thrusting though, dragging it out for me, and somehow starting to drive me back upward again. As soon as he felt the switch, he knifed up, throwing me back down onto my back and sitting back on his heels. He grabbed my legs, pushing my knees back into my chest and settling my silly TARDIS-sock-clad feet onto his chest. He looked down, as if seeing them for the first time, and smiled big, his finger stroking over the side of my foot. "Never change, Pip," he said warmly as his cock slammed inside me, hard.

My head fell back and my mouth opened to let out a loud moan, too far gone to think about the consequences of that. But Adam's hand slammed down onto my mouth and stayed there as he started thrusting into me- fast, hard, unrelenting, not giving me the chance to even pull in a proper breath as I felt myself climb toward an orgasm faster than I knew was possible.

It slammed through me just a short couple moments later, making my feet slam into his chest and he let out a grunt at the impact, but kept pounding into me through it all.

As soon as the last wave moved out of me, his tense voice said oddly, "Want to see something cool?" he asked, then his cock pulled completely out of me and two fingers thrust inside, turning, and raking over my top wall, working my G-spot with expert precision, fast, almost frantic, until just maybe a minute later, another wave crashed through my system, making my entire body writhe on the bed, my cries a muffled sound against his hand.

He smiled when my body relaxed and he slid back inside me, this time slowly, like he had all the time in the world. "That was three," he said, giving me a small, sweet smile. "I think I owe you one more."

And then his body pressed down over mine. His hand moved from my mouth. "I want to hear you," he said quietly near my ear as he moved gently inside me, unhurried, sweet. Making love to me again and I had to bury my face in his neck, eyes closed tight against the tears that threatened.

And as the fourth orgasm rolled through me, slow, deep, overwhelming to my system, my voice caught on a hitch as I cried out his name, two tears slipping down my cheeks as I held onto him while he tensed, murmured my name against my shoulder, and came with me.

His body weight came down on me after, a welcome feeling as I struggled to pull myself back together because he had pulled me apart at my seams.

We stayed that way for a long time after, him still inside me, the sweat drying, our hearts slowing, our breathing evening out.

A while later, but way too soon, he shifted up, kissing me slow and deep for a long minute before sliding out of me and pulling his pants back up.

"I'll be right back," he said and I knew he had to run downstairs to deal with the condom.

Which was good.

I needed a minute.

Or an hour.

Or what was left of my lifetime to pull myself back together.

I took a few deep breaths, swatting at the tears, knowing there was a time and a place for them and that this was most definitely not it. I sat up, fetched my clothes and threw them into my suitcase, pulling out fresh ones-yoga pants and a heavy blue sweater, and slipping into them.

I moved back onto my bed, climbing half under the covers and waiting.

And waiting.

And waiting.

Just when I was starting to think he wasn't coming back, I heard footsteps on the stairs and then across the floor. Adam moved into the doorway, a white tee on where it hadn't been when he left, and two steaming cups in his hands.

"If I am going to deprive you of sleep and then steal all your energy stores," he started with a cocky little grin that was way too sweet when sent in my direction, especially after having had my energy stores stolen from him an impossible four times, "I better caffeinate you."

"Solid plan," I said, taking my tea from him and holding it between my hands, letting it burn into me slightly, letting that keep me grounded as he climbed into bed with me, sitting up against the headboard, our shoulders brushing.

It was so casually intimate, so easy, like we had been doing it every morning for years.

We stayed oddly, tensely silent though, both of us lost in our own thoughts for an uncomfortably long time before Adam finally broke it.

"There's so much that needs to be said here," he said and I closed my eyes tight, taking a deep breath. "But I don't think anything we could say would change this."

He was right.

We could talk for hours about how much we wished we had more time, how it sucked that we lost the years, that it was nice to be able to come together, that it sucked that it was all there was for us.

But all that wouldn't alter the fact that I had to leave, that I had a life to get back to, that all we had was one blissful, perfect holiday to look back on fondly.

"Callie, come on down and get some food before your flight," my mother called from downstairs, perfectly timed because I wasn't sure how much longer I could keep it together while alone with him.

"So it starts," Adam said and, if I wasn't mistaken, regret was plain in his voice as he climbed out of my bed.

I climbed out too, going over to my suitcase and shoving the half-bursting contents back in so I could zip it. When I stood back up, Adam moved in and took it from me. "Thanks," I said, feeling a bit awkward as I turned to grab my messenger bag and purse.

I stripped my bed and put the sheets in the hamper.

When I moved toward the doorway, I looked back at my room with a feeling of longing.

But I locked those feelings inside along with the love for Adam and the regret of years lost and told myself to only open that box up again when I felt strong enough to deal with them.

Which might be never.

And, hell, that worked for me too.

Breakfast was eaten.

Amy left.

Then I said goodbye to my mother and brother as my father took my bags to the car.

My mother, the keen woman she was, made up some lame reason to need to see my brother in the living room and pulled him out of the kitchen with her, the kitchen where Adam had been trying to catch my eye for half an hour and I had been trying really hard to avoid it.

I was still studying my feet when I felt my cup pulled from my hands and heard it click down on the counter. Adam's body moved close to mine as his hands slid across my jaw to frame my face, tilting it up.

I took a breath and let my eyes find his.

His lips parted as though he was about to say something, but instead, he let his face lower and kissed me slow, soft.

He kissed me goodbye.

Then his forehead pressed into mine for a long moment.

"I'll see you at Christmas, Pip," he told me, releasing my face, stepping away, then leaving the room.

Adam never showed up for Christmas.

But he planned to be there this year.

For what? For me?

Was I just some holiday fling to him now? Don't see me ninety percent of the time but expect me to fall into bed on Thanksgiving, Christmas, and Easter?

That, well, that was unacceptable if that was what he was thinking.

Granted, a part of me, even a pretty large part, wanted him for whatever small piece of his life he would give me. But the other part knew that I couldn't handle that. I wouldn't survive an on and off soaring high followed by a crippling low when it was over again.

"Cal, we're going to be late," my father said, startling me out of my thoughts, standing in the open back doorway.

"Right," I said with a nod as I followed him out.

I had a nice drive to the airport and a flight home to think and over-think and make myself half-sick about the whole situation before I made it back to my apartment, letting Albus out of his carrier, shaking my head at the dirty cat-look he sent me, and going into my room to unpack. If there was one thing I knew that helped ease some of my chronic obsessive thinking, it was keeping busy.

So I took all my toiletries back to the bathroom.

I grabbed a laundry basket for all my dirty clothes from the trip.

I put my suitcase up on the bed and unzipped it.

And it was then that I realized Adam hadn't taken my bag out of sheer chivalry.

He took it because he had put something inside of it.

And what did he put?

A family size bag of plain potato chips.

My ass hit my bed as a small sob escaped my lips.

Then I did exactly what any woman in my situation would do; I devoured that entire bag of chips. And when that didn't quite seem to numb the pain, I tried half a gallon of ice cream.

I showered.

I slept in short spells.

Then I tried to get on with my life.

Adam

"Adam, get your head in the game, man," Cory demanded, waving his hand with the racquet out, frustrated with my preoccupation.

We had been at the racquetball court for almost forty minutes and I had been lost in my own thoughts pretty much the entire time, making the very competitive Cory lose his patience with me.

"Brought you here to get out of that shit mood of yours, not watch you drown in it."

He was right.

I had agreed to come because I knew that activity usually worked to clear my mind.

It had been a week since I watched Callie drive away. Only after having her for a few days.

And the overall feeling I had as she left was: not enough.

I always kind of figured that if we finally gave in to the unresolved feelings we had toward each other, that it would finally clear my mind of her. I always figured the way she hung around in the back of my mind was because it felt like a missed opportunity, the curiosity of the unknown.

But now that I had both literally and figuratively gotten a taste, yeah, I found I needed more. I needed it all.

I just couldn't have it.

I remember reading something in philosophy class in college about how it was impossible to step into the same river twice, that opportunities lost were lost for good. At the time, the wisdom fell on deaf ears. But I truly understood the phrase after Callie walked back out of my life.

I couldn't help but feel like we missed our shot.

Her life was in D.C.

My life was in Massachusetts.

And we both deserved better than to just screw on the rare occasion we saw each other, no matter how strong the urge was.

And the urge *would* be strong. Because sex with Callie was nothing like the sex I had had with other women in my life. It was more. It was, in an odd way, meaningful.

"You gonna tell me what this is about?" Cory asked, dropping the racquet and leaning against the wall.

"You don't want to know," I said honestly, dropping my own racquet and turning away from him.

"This is about Callie, isn't it?"

I stopped dead mid-stride, everything inside and out getting tense as I slowly turned. "What?"

Cory's smile was slow and knowing as his head shook. "Please, Adam. I'm not blind. I'm pretty sure you stopped breathing when she walked into that kitchen. It was some straight out of a fairy tale shit."

"Cor..." I said, running a hand across the back of my neck, knowing that if there was one rule of guy code you didn't screw with, it was the one about not putting your hands on your buddy's little sister.

He shrugged his shoulder, giving me a small smile. "Man, she has had a thing for you since she was little. Figured you always saw her as a little sister until I saw your face when she walked into that kitchen the other day."

"I know I should have..."

"What? Asked for permission?" he asked, smiling big. "Callie is a big girl. She can make her own decisions." That was typical Cory- carefree, easy-going. "So I'm right. Callie has you being a moody shit. What happened?"

"She left," I said before I could stop the words from coming out.

His smile slowly fell, his gaze going to the floor for a second. "So this isn't some new development? You have feelings for her? I mean, aside from caring for her because you've known her your whole life."

"Yeah, I have feelings for her."

"Shit," he said, shaking his head. "This puts me in a weird position. Because, as your friend, I need to tell you that if you have finally found the woman who puts you in a shit mood for a week just because she's not around, that you'd be an idiot to not try to find a way to give it a shot. On the other hand, as her big brother, I feel the need to tell you that if you so much as bruise that sweet little nerdy heart of hers, that I will make you regret it."

"I appreciate the support and you know I'd never hurt Cal. But fact of the matter is, Cor, we have two different lives."

He seemed to completely ignore that. "You showed her your house the day after Thanksgiving, didn't you?" he asked and I nodded. "You had to have known that that was her dream home, right? What'd she say?"

"That I should have used wallpaper instead of paint in the bedroom."

He snorted at that. "I am going to go ahead and ignore the fact that you showed my baby sister your bedroom. Did she have a shitfit over that library?"

I never showed her the library, I realized with a start.

After bringing her up to my room, a place I had started to think I would never get to see her, and being able to indulge a fantasy that had plagued me at night for years, I had completely forgotten.

Fact of the matter was, shit changed up in that bedroom, when I got my mouth on her, when I got inside her. And, judging by the way she reacted afterward, she felt it too and was trying to keep those feelings in check.

I was trying to do the same.

So I had tried to get her out of there as soon as possible, forgetting in the process to show her a room that was all but useless to me, but she would melt over. It had been, after the master suite, the only other room that was completely finished. I had sanded and re-stained all the floor-to-ceiling bookshelves and refinished the floors and bought an executive desk and a chaise lounge to decorate it.

The shelves themselves, aside from my small collection of books, were all but empty.

"Amy called. We had to head out before she could see the whole house."

"You know, I guess I've always found that house thing weird."

"The house thing?" I repeated.

"You could have bought one of those new townhouses. Or something more modern, something that didn't need so much work. You work a lot. You don't have the time for that shit. But you picked her house instead. Interesting, that."

"When did you become a sap?"

"Oh, about ten minutes ago when I realized my baby sister and my best friend have been in love with each other since they were teens, whether they realized it or not. That's some straight-up Disney shit right there."

"You're still forgetting the part about how we can't be together."

"Right. The pissy mood factor. Well, way I see it, things are looking up on that front."

"What do you mean?"

"I talked to mom this morning. Apparently, her first day back, she walked into layoffs."

"She lost her job?" I asked, feeling my stomach tighten, knowing how worried she was about that seeming inevitability. She was a creature of habit. She liked consistency. She got stressed out when big changes came around. Granted, everyone knew she wasn't crazy about her job.

It wasn't her dream.

In college, she had majored in literature. Then, to appease her worried mother, minored in graphic design, for which she had a fair amount of skill but very little passion for. But, literature being a somewhat useless degree unless you went and got your doctorate to eventually teach it at a college level, she had quickly found a job in graphic design. And that was where she had been since about a week after graduation. It was what she knew. And it was safe and steady.

Callie liked safe and steady.

"Hey, maybe you should start viewing her misfortune as your golden opportunity."

"How so?"

He rolled his eyes at me as the next set of guys moved into the room to play. Realizing our time was up, we moved out and headed back out toward the rest of the gym. "What, I have to spell it all out for you? Cal is not the kind of girl who lives in D.C. She's small town, not big city. And D.C. is expensive when you're out of work. All she needs is a little push..."

"To move back here."

"Exactly."

It wasn't a bad plan.

Cory was right; Callie was in D.C. because it was the first place she found a job. She wasn't in love with the restaurants and nightlife. She was never that kind of girl to begin with. I doubted she had even seen the inside of one of the bars there. And the only stores she likely frequented were the essentials and the bookstores. The rest of the time, I imagined, she spent holed up in her apartment.

"I can't ask her to move in with me, Cor," I said, snorting a little at the idea. "True, we've known each other since she was born, but not that way."

He laughed at that as we moved out into the parking lot of the gym. "What is 'that way' anyway? The shit you get to know about a partner, sex aside, is the same shit you know about your friends- favorite colors, movies, food preferences, political beliefs, how you just...

click. You know all that shit about Cal and you always have. I think you're overestimating how long it is going to take you two to get serious if she is in the area."

"So you're saying..."

"That Ma already offered to let her crash for as long as she needs to figure shit out. She's rooting for you two."

"She wasn't exactly subtle about my room placement or asking us to drop Pops off."

"I think she was just waiting for you to get your head out of your ass and notice her. But then she went away and didn't come back enough. Ruined her dreams of having you join the family in a legal kind of way."

"Yeah, she would finally have a son she could be proud of," I joked, smiling big when he threw his bottle of water at me.

"Fuck off," he said, retrieving it then unlocking his car. I leaned against mine as he turned back. "So, now that you got that shit out of your system, you can stop being such a whiny bitch and do something about the situation."

"Nice to know I got your blessing," I laughed, shaking my head.

"The threat still stands. Hurt that girl and I'll burn that fixer-upper of yours to the fucking ground. Back here tomorrow, same time, and bring your A-game for a change," he said, sliding into his car, turning it over, and pulling away.

I got into my own car and drove back to that fixer-upper of mine, going into the library and pouring myself a drink, running over the developments of that afternoon.

First, Cory not only knew about me and Callie, but was on-board with the whole situation. So was his mother. As for their father, well, that was an unknown. It was hard to get a read on him. But I did know one thing, he thought that that girl was the sole reason the sun came up every morning. She was more him than Cory was, the two of them always close, always discussing books and philosophies. That being said, I had always been like another son to the family. And he knew me well enough to know that my intentions were genuine. I wouldn't risk my relationships with all of them for some quick tail or a silly fling. They were the closest thing I had to family left.

As much as I wasn't happy that she lost her job, Cory was right, it was the perfect opportunity. That was, if she was willing to move back home after so much time. It was one thing to move back with your parents directly after college, it was another to move back after you had been living on your own for a while.

I finished my drink and headed upstairs toward the master suite, going into the bath I never got to show to Callie either. I had replaced all the old, ugly tile the house had come with that must have been replaced in the fifties with warm cream tile, a giant glass walk-in shower, and a large vintage-looking but brand new soaking tub.

I climbed into the shower and weighed the options.

Sure, I could sit back and wait for the chips to fall where I wanted them to, wait for Callie to make the decision to move back home.

But, that being said, if she was freaking out, there was a chance she had already applied to a dozen jobs and might take whatever the first one that came her way was.

It wasn't worth the risk.

Besides that, I knew Callie. Whether she wanted to admit it or not, she was a romantic. No one went for a degree in literature and hated the idea of love. Not with all the Bronte, Austen, and Hardy they bury their noses in.

If ever there was a woman who would appreciate and was deserving of a grand romantic gesture, it was her.

On that note, I threw on some fresh clothes, went back into my room, sat on the side of the bed, picked up my cell, and called Cory.

"Yeah?"

"Any idea where I can find some packing boxes and bubble wrap?"

Callie

It was a hell of a Monday following Thanksgiving weekend.

First, of course, there was the fact that I was not in the best of spirits after coming back home. Add in the fact that I barely slept and when I finally did pass out, I overslept so I had to rush through my twenty-minute morning routine in five, leaving me running up the street toward my office building in the pouring rain, half-blind because my glasses were covered in raindrops.

Then, chilled to the bone, hair a sopping mess, I rode the elevator up with one of the accounting guys who always looked at me like he had X-ray eyes and, that particular morning, knew just how cold-hardened my nipples were.

And then, coup de grace, I barely sat down at my desk, wiping my glasses with a tissue, when the girl from HR came up to speak to me.

I wasn't prepared.

I should have been prepared.

But my mind was on half a dozen other things.

So I didn't notice the things my mother had

warned me about when we had had our talk. Like how some of the desks were empty. And, when I really focused, there were faces standing around that I had never seen before.

They weren't new employees.

Oh, no.

See, she told me that when companies were going belly-up and doing large amounts of layoffs, they almost never did the tasks themselves. They farmed out the dirty work. They called in people who fired people for a living, people who knew exactly what to say so people didn't blow their tops and start breaking stuff or falling into hysterics.

I was led into the conference room where a man and a woman in bland suits with bland features and bland voices invited me to sit down.

I sat down across the long table from them where I found a company folder already awaiting me.

Then I was thanked for my hard work, told that it was not a reflection of my work performance, and laid off.

I took my folder that offered me a six-week severance package and a letter of recommendation, and was led back toward my desk where I was handed a sturdy paper stock box and watched by the HR lady as I emptied my desk of my personal items. That included two hardcover books, three paperbacks, a picture of my parents, an assorted array of colored pencils, and a tiny little pig figurine.

"Best of luck, Carlie," the HR lady said, making me wince.

They had taken years of my life, given me six

weeks of pay, and they didn't even know my name.

I stopped at the corner store on my way home.

But I didn't pick up chips.

Chips were for panic attacks.

Ice cream was for depression.

I headed straight to the freezer section with a hand cart and grabbed three gallons- vanilla bean, triple chocolate, and just to cover my bases, rocky road. Then I dragged myself back to the apartment that I knew I would no longer be able to afford in two months, took a long hot shower, changed into the baggiest, oldest sweats I owned, put on mindless TV, and dove so deep into the frozen deliciousness that by the time I realized I was still eating it, half of the vanilla, half of the chocolate, and a quarter of the rocky road was already gone.

Stomach aching, matching the feeling in my chest in a way that made my whole center hurt, I climbed into bed and passed out.

The next morning, I finished the damage I started on the ice cream, then ordered a giant salad out of guilt, eating it while I did what I knew I needed to do, I called my mother and told her what happened.

See, while she absolutely *had* told me so, she didn't remind me of that fact.

Instead, she just went ahead and was the great mom I had been blessed with my whole life. She gave me tips for my resume. She reminded me that if I was thinking of changing career paths, this was the right opportunity for that. Then, as if all that wasn't enough, she offered to let me come home.

At first, that idea filled me with a rush of longing and relief.

It was a simple, temporary solution to a complicated, long-term problem.

I, unlike most of the grads I knew, never moved back home, never got that leg up that came from having a roof over my head and food on my table while I built up a savings to get myself into a better situation. My mother raised me to be self-sufficient so it felt like defeat to move home when I knew I could be working and providing for myself.

It would be a smart move to go back, not blow through my savings paying rent while I looked for a new job.

But, I worried, more so... the reason I wanted so badly to move back had nothing to do with it being a wise decision financially, but everything to do with being closer to Adam. And that, well, I wasn't sure I could let myself be that needy, that sad, that pathetic.

Besides, he didn't show any interest in that.

We had a fling.

He got me out of his system.

Case closed.

So, as much as it was the better choice for me, I wasn't going to move back home. I was going to drown in ice cream and potato chips while I applied to every single graphic design gig in D.C. Which, well, was a lot. I could even just do contract jobs to hold me over until I found something more permanent. My rent was already paid up for December and my severance package would pay it for January. That gave me plenty of time to figure something out. It wasn't like I had some high-paying job and needed to be picky about what I took. I had an entry-level graphic design job that paid me pitifully little, so little that I actually had a book budget. In my ledger next to my rent, water, electricity, subscription TV services, car insurance, and grocery shopping money, there was a line dedicated to how much I had available to me to buy books. And it wasn't nearly enough. So, yeah, getting another low paying job that I wasn't crazy about, it wouldn't be a problem.

After just a couple days or weeks of stress-inducing interviews and waiting to hear back from them, life would settle back down to normal.

And as I sat at my laptop clicking through the want ads online, I tried really hard to ignore the voice inside my head that said "normal" wasn't good enough.

I had never been unhappy. Not really.

I worked hard like I was raised to do. I was a good employee. I paid my bills on time. I never overdrafted my bank account. I put small amounts into savings every month. I spent my free time reading and watching shows and movies I loved. Occasionally, I dated. It had always seemed like enough.

But, fact of the matter was, something had changed.

Maybe it was as simple as going back home and spending time with my family, seeing my father happy with his career path, my mother with hers, my brother, my cousin, Adam. Everyone seemed to be doing what they wanted. While I worked a job I was good at but did nothing for me. I had few friends. My family was hours and hours away. I hadn't had even a casual-type relationship in almost a year.

So being around family and old friends, having some time with a man, it all made me see something I hadn't even realized.

I was lonely.

I was so all-consumingly lonely that it made my chest feel constricted. It made my bed feel way too big. It made the world seem larger than it used to, more hollow.

I sighed, slamming the lid to my laptop and bringing my ice cream back to the freezer.

Four digital applications seemed like enough for the day. There were at least seventy-five of them already swirling around out there waiting to be responded to. It had only been a week. I was way ahead of most recently unemployed people. Hell, most people probably took the whole first week to sleep in, binge-watch TV they had missed, let loose a little. So there was no reason to feel guilty when I went into my bathroom and filled up the tub then climbed in with a book.

And then there was no reason to feel guilty when the water turned cold, I drained the tub, got changed into more hideously oversized sweat clothes, and took the book to my couch with me.

There wasn't even any reason to feel guilty when I fell asleep with the book in my hand on my couch at three o'clock in the afternoon on a Tuesday.

I was startled awake by knocking on my apartment door.

Maybe 'startled' wasn't the right word.

I woke up with my heart lodged in my throat, inwardly suppressing the urge to ninja roll across my apartment floor and go hide in my bedroom.

No one knocked on my door.

In the couple of years since I moved in, literally not once had someone knocked on my door.

I carefully bookmarked my book, placing it down on the coffee table as I moved across the apartment, grabbing the giant R2-D2 paperweight off the small mail table I kept beside my door, and leaned up to look out the peephole.

But all I saw was the hall.

And the knocking had stopped a good full minute before.

Curious, I unlocked the deadbolt, but left the chain on, pulling the door open to peek out the crack.

"You don't ask who it is before you open the door, Pip?"

Callie

I'm pretty sure a mass murderer standing in my hall with a giant, bloody katana, and a severed head in his hand would have somehow been less surprising than Adam standing there.

I could only see a sliver of him through the gap in the door, gray slacks and a black dress shirt.

"I promise I'm not here to kill you. You can take the chain off the door," he said, sounding amused and I snapped back, shaking some sense back into my head. I closed the door, slid the chain, then had a momentary freak out about the fact that my gray sweatshirt was about four sizes too big with a couple bleach stains and that my sweatpants were printed with parrots and I had mismatched patterned socks on and that my hair had probably dried into an absolute wavy mess, but just as quickly realized there was nothing I could do about that.

So I pulled the door open to reveal the perfectly dressed Adam with his perfect face and perfect hair and perfect teasing smile as his eyes lowered to my hand where I was still holding R2-D2.

"Gonna bash my skull in with a *Star Trek* toy?"

"*Wars*," I corrected automatically. "*Star Wars*."

The smile only widened at that.

When he didn't say anything, I shook my head a little. "Adam, what are you doing here?"

"Well," he said, looking very much like he was up to something as he rocked back on his heels, tucking his hands into his pockets. "I heard about the job thing," he said. "I'm sorry, Cal."

"You don't look sorry," I said, brows drawing together because he was doing his damndest to hold a smile back.

"Yeah, I'm really not," he said, letting the smile free. "I'm sorry that you're stressed out about it, but I'm not sorry it happened."

"Ah... okay," I said, brows knitted, not understanding why he was smiling about my misfortune.

"Ask me why I'm here again, Cal."

"Why are you here?"

He moved to the side and I heard a sliding noise just a second before he pulled a large stack of folded cardboard moving boxes in front of him. "We're having a packing party," he informed me.

"A packing party? I'm not packing anything."

"Well, if you'd rather leave everything you own behind..." he said, shrugging.

"Adam, I'm not going anywhere."

"Sure you are. You are coming back to Massachusetts and stocking all your stuff in the living space outside of your bedroom. You, however, I think will be spending most of your nights in my bed."

I'm pretty sure something had happened to me. Like maybe my bathroom radio had fallen into the bath and electrocuted me and I was having that thing they say people have right before they die, when their brains misfire and give you happy images that many people associate with an afterlife.

Because there was no way that Adam Gallagher was standing in my hallway with moving boxes and telling me to move back home so he could have me in his bed at night.

"See, I knew I would need these," he said, moving to put the boxes back against the wall and I heard a plastic bag rustling. Then he lifted his arms and showed me four shopping bags full of, you guessed it, potato chips. "Come on, let me in, Pip," he said as he moved forward.

And, still not entirely convinced I wasn't dying by electrocution, I moved out of the way and watched as he moved inside my apartment, stopping short, looking around, then depositing the chips onto my coffee table and then turning back to me with a smile.

"So where's your wand?"

Okay. So maybe my apartment was a bit nerd-chic.

I had made sure it was respectably adult-ish in that I had a nice, tufted gray couch, a distressed white coffee table, throw pillows, spot rugs, and curtains on my windows. But if you looked, there was a touch of some nerd everywhere. My bookshelves that lined the whole wall in my living room were actually Tetris-shaped. The artwork on my walls was actually framed quotes from Bronte sister novels. My shower curtain had the periodic table of elements, and pretty much every hard surface had some knick-knack from some TV show or movie or book.

And suddenly I felt very insecure at the idea of Adam seeing all those things.

I picked up a hand and waved toward the bookshelf where all the *Harry Potter* books were on display.

"Are those Tetris blocks?" he asked, smiling wider. "And... is that a floppy disk throw pillow?" He looked over at me, likely taking in the none-too-subtle embarrassment and shaking his head. "I'm not teasing you, Pip. I like that this place looks like you live here. Most houses have no personality anymore."

"Um, Adam, why is there..." I said, looking out toward the hallway where, butted up against the huge supply of boxes, there was a small suitcase.

"Well," he said, coming up behind me, folding his arms over my belly. "You have a lot of stuff. I figure it will take a couple days to get it all boxed up. Plus, you know..." he said, turning his face and kissing my neck. "I think we are going to find ourselves constantly distracted."

"By what?"

"Oh," he said, his hand sliding lower, almost indecently so, "I think we can figure that out," he promised in a low, smooth voice.

I looked over at the moving boxes again, shaking my head to try to clear it. "Okay," I said, trying for firm and mostly hitting the mark. "Okay. Off," I said, grabbing his wrists and pushing down until he released me with a small chuckle. "Okay. You need to deal with that," I said, waving a hand into the hallway.

And I needed to dive into a bag of those chips.

After I got into less ridiculous clothes. And brushed my teeth. And made sure my body wasn't floating in my bathtub.

"I'll be right back," I said, rushing off to my bedroom and closing the door, taking a deep breath.

Adam was in my apartment.

Adam was in my apartment with every intention of helping me pack up everything I owned and bringing me back to Massachusetts with him where he expected me to fall into bed with him.

And, well, I had no idea how I was supposed to feel about that.

I heard the front door close and was acutely aware of the fact that he was likely inspecting every inch of my living room, dining room, and kitchen. He would find nothing in my fridge but some bottle of white wine work gave me the Christmas before, sitting there because I didn't like white, and a plastic carton of baby spinach. The freezer, however, was loaded with ice cream and frozen pizzas. My sink was half-full of dishes. There was a pile of shoes behind my front door. And there were at least four different sweatshirts in various places like the back of my couch, hanging off one of my kitchen cabinets, and at least two somewhere near the door.

But that would have to wait.

Ratty old sweat clothes and stale breath needed to be dealt with first.

I ripped off my sweatshirt on my way to the bathroom, putting toothpaste on my brush and brushing as I went to my closet and pulled on a slightly better fitting long-sleeve black tee. I slipped out of my ugly sweatpants and changed into more acceptable yoga ones. Then I went back to my bathroom, rinsed, and finger-combed my hair into order.

"Hey, Pip, you have to come out eventually," Adam called through my bedroom door as I stared at it, trying to convince myself to walk out.

"I'm coming," I said, lying.

But it was time to stop stalling.

Before I could cross the room, the knob turned and the door pushed open. And there he was, stepping into my bedroom.

He took me in for a moment before his eyes moved around, landing on my very pink comforter with my pile of books on the empty side. "Come over here," he said, moving his head to the side, eyes a little heavy.

Okay.

So being beckoned by the guy you had been in love with for pretty much your entire life after believing for years that nothing could ever happen between you, yeah, it was pretty much a dream come true.

And, having had first hand experience at how much better he was in reality than fantasy, my libido was trying to take control and let me throw myself at him.

But we needed to talk.

"Adam..."

"Uh-oh," he said, smiling again. "Serious voice."

"Well, this is a serious topic. I'm not moving, Adam. I'm looking for jobs here."

"In graphic design."

"It's what I went to school for."

"You went to school for literature. Graphic design was your safety net. It was supposed to be something to get you by until you found what you really wanted to do." He took a couple steps further, making me have to resist the urge to retreat. "You can't live a life inside a safety net, Cal."

"I can sure try," I said, smiling because I knew

he was right.

He smiled back, but smaller. "I get that you get nervous when things start changing or are out of your control. But you have to see that this, us getting together, then you losing your job, then your parents offering you to stay while you figured things out... you have to see this as fate."

"Fate?" I asked, trying to not believe it, not wanting to set myself up for something that might not happen, not willing to let my feelings for him out of that tightly locked box inside until I was sure it was safe. "That's a little..."

"Don't do that. Girls who have loved a guy since they were both kids don't throw it in his face when he shows up and says he feels the same way."

And right then, those feelings I had, yeah they round kicked out of that mother effing box.

"Did you just..."

"Loved you even when I shouldn't have, Pip," he said, moving across the floor toward me. "Maybe life happened and it got pushed to the back of my mind, but it was always there. I just didn't realize it until you walked into that kitchen again. But it all came back with you standing there. You know, I worried growing up would change you, would make you into someone different than who I knew all my life. But you're the same girl, Callie. Just with a little more life experience and a slight potato chip addiction."

A snorting laugh escaped me at that, glad he put some levity into an otherwise scarily intense declaration.

Because, fact of the matter was, it was one thing to feel that way yourself. It was a complete other to realize the person you felt that for, felt that way for you as well.

"You love me?" I asked, shaking my head at him.

"Yeah, Cal. You love me too," he said, his body moving into mine, his fingers gliding up my arm then over my shoulder to settle at my jaw. "Come on. Admit it."

"I love you too," I admitted, because, well, I did.

"So, you see why it would be stupid to keep putting out applications in D.C. when we both know what you really want is to come back to Massachusetts with me and give this a shot."

I did. I did see that.

"But there are more job opportunities here," I reasoned.

"I don't exactly live in the boonies, Pip. There are places to work by me."

That was also true. He, my parents, my brother, and even my cousin all had good jobs in my hometown. Granted, all in varying fields. But that being said, any company with any level of success employed graphic designers.

"In fact," he went on, both of his hands moving to cross over my lower back, pulling my body flush to his so that I needed to arch backward to keep looking at his face, "you know who I happen to know?"

"I'm sure you're about to tell me," I said with a small smile.

"Emily Andrews. And Emily happens to run a small indie publishing house." I felt my heart start to pound hard in my chest, making my pulse beat in unusual places- my temples, my throat, my wrists. "And when I talked to Emily, she said she happens to be in the market for new editors. That literature degree of yours that everyone thought was so useless... it happens to make you qualified to edit."

No.

No freaking way.

No way was he friends with someone who could give me every book lovers dream job.

"Alright, breathe, Pip," he said, chuckling slightly.

"You got me a job?" I asked, my voice a strange, croaking sound.

"Well," he said, shrugging a little. "I got you an interview. The convincing her to hire you thing is up to you. Though, I have complete faith that you will nerd-talk her into it."

"Okay. I think I need to sit down," I said, my head literally feeling like it was spinning, putting all previous issues with vertigo to complete shame.

Adam's arms squeezed me tighter. "I got you," he said, refusing to let me go. "It's everything you've ever wanted, Cal."

He was right.

I had always wanted a job that coincided with my love of books.

And I had always wanted Adam.

But somehow, inexplicably, having all my dreams come true was proving to be one of the scariest feelings I had ever known. Maybe because getting all you ever wanted meant that there was a chance you could *lose* it all as well. In a way, it was easier and safer to never reach for those things, to never know what it felt like to hold them and then feel them possibly slip through your fingers some day.

"Alright, what's going on in there?" Adam asked, reaching up and tapping the center of my forehead.

I let out a slow breath and gave him the truth. "I'm scared."

"Of what?"

"Getting everything I want and losing it again."

Adam nodded a little, understanding that. "Look. A job, even a dream job, is just a job. It's replaceable. For every position you lose, there are a dozen others you could find. And me, well, I can't guarantee that we will live happily ever after. But I can promise you one thing, Pip," he said, leaning his head down, eyes intense, tone sincere, "you're never going to lose me." He let that sink in. And it did, down to my marrow. "Besides, I am under a threat to not hurt you by Cor."

I felt my lips tip up at that idea, Cory never being the kind of brother to threaten boyfriends. He just wasn't that type. "What did he threaten you with?"

"Arson. He will burn down my house," he said, grinning.

"Why would he punish m*e* for you being an ass?" I asked. "I love that house."

"Knew you would. And when you come back, you can actually see more of it than the foyer, hallway, and master bedroom."

"You better not have screwed up that library," I warned.

"Just restored the wood. I think I only have enough books to fill one shelf."

"That's blasphemous," I said, hands sliding up the material of his shirt, arms folding across the back of his neck.

"Luckily for me, I know this girl who knows a lot about books..."

I returned the warm smile he gave me, my heart swelling wide in my chest, the sensation so perfect it was almost painful. I went up on my toes as my arms pulled his head down toward me, my lips sealing over his, kissing him with every bit of happiness, confusion, excitement, and fear inside my body.

His hands moved down, grabbing my behind and squeezing, pulling my hips against his where I felt his hard cock press into my stomach. A needy moan escaped my lips, muffled by his. Adam's fingers slid upward, snagging the hem of my shirt and dragging it up. My lips ripped from his so he could free me of the material; my hands going to his buttons to do the same for him.

His hands went to my hips, turning me, and pulling my back against his solid chest, his hands whispering up my belly to cup my breasts, his fingers pinching and rolling my nipples until I shamelessly rubbed my ass against his cock, begging for relief from the torture. He released my breasts, his hands grabbing my pants and panties and dragging them halfway down my legs, giving me a second to step out before his palm cupped my sex, making my legs get shaky for a moment. I had to bring my arms up to wrap around the back of his neck to keep my feet as his thumb moved up to start stroking over my clit. His middle finger moved down my cleft and slid inside me, a deep, low, rumbling sound vibrating from his chest.

"Drenched for me," he said, nipping into my earlobe.

"Adam, please," I begged, grinding down onto his hand.

"Please what?" he asked, voice a sexy grumble.

There was a time for making love.

There was a time for sex.

And sometimes, well, it was time for something else.

"Please fuck me," I demanded, cheeks heating a little at using those words, and especially using them with him.

There was a low, growling sound in his chest in response, his hand leaving my sex as his other hand moved to my shoulder and bent me forward toward my bed. My hands met the soft material of my girly comforter, my knees hitting the edge of the mattress, my ass in the air toward him.

I heard the zip of his pants, the ripping of a condom wrapper, then felt his body move in behind me. His fingers slid down my sides over my ribs, making me shiver, then up over my ass, before I felt his legs cage mine in on the mattress. The head of his cock pressed between my thighs, sliding up my slick cleft and rubbing over my clit as my hips slammed back into him, needy, greedy for the feel of him inside me again.

His cock slid backward and pressed against the opening to my body, just creating pressure for a long moment, until my hands curled into the sheets, until my hips started grinding against him, until I let out a loud whimper.

Before the sound was even fully out of my

throat, Adam thrust forward, his cock slamming impossibly deep.

"Oh my God," I moaned.

His fingers dug into my hipbones, borderline painful.

There was no teasing, no build up.

He pounded into me hard, deep, fast, using my hips to slam deeper, yanking me backward each time he thrust forward.

"Mine," he growled, his pace getting faster somehow, my moans louder and more desperate by the second. "Finally fucking mine."

I was.

But I always had been.

"Adam... I..."

The orgasm ripped almost violently through my system, making me collapse forward onto the bed, body completely boneless and the waves kept crashing through me, my cries loud enough to disturb all my neighbors as Adam's body came down on mine, still thrusting until my body went completely slack and he came on a hiss.

"Fuck," he said a minute later, lifting up his weight that had been crushing me. "Sorry," he said, nipping into my shoulder as he slowly slid out of me, gently slapping my ass as he moved into my bathroom.

The low, short chuckle was all the proof I needed that he had seen my periodic table of elements shower curtain. He walked back out, his pants back up his legs, but left unzipped, making them sling almost indecently low on his hips. Chest just a little sweaty, hair just a little more rumpled than it usually was, he was the sexiest thing I had ever seen in my life.

His eyes moved over me, making me painfully aware of my nakedness, but my body too sated to do anything about it.

"I could get used to seeing you like this," he told me, sitting down beside me then laying back, tapping his chest. And, well, I didn't need any more encouragement than that. I pushed up on wobbly arms and rested my head on his shoulder, my chest on his chest. His arms went around me, one stroking through my hair, the other resting across my hips. "So?" he asked a long couple of minutes later, my eyes getting heavy.

"So?" I repeated, tilting my head to look at his profile.

"So are you going to stop being chickenshit and take the leap or what?"

"I'm not chickenshit. I'm... cautious," I objected.

"Use whatever synonym you want, Pip. It all just means scared."

He wasn't wrong. "I just want to make sure we both know what we're getting into."

"Cal, I literally know just about everything there is to know about you from how it took you until you were nine to give a bike without training wheels a try. Then, after falling off six days in a row, declaring that people were no more meant to ride on two wheels than fish were to walk on land and that you were never getting on your bike again. I know how you claimed to stage an anti-Valentine's Day protest every February, but you actually holed up in your father's study and read *Pride and Prejudice* for the umpteenth time. I know you hate mangoes and love junk food. I know that the first time you got drunk was when you were sixteen and that Cory had to come pick you up from where you were sitting inside a bathroom at the house of one of the kids you went to school with a fucking macaw that you named Paulie even though he kept telling you over and over that his name was Magoo..."

"Magoo is a stupid name for a parrot."

"And then when Cory opened the door and asked you why you were with a parrot in the bathroom instead of socializing with the kids your age, you declared the bird was smarter than the whole lot of them and was a better conversationalist. And then..."

"You can stop there," I said, eyes huge, knowing the story that, while it started funny, went downhill from there.

"And then you threw up, cursed tequila to the devil, and cried the whole way back to your parents' saying you were such a disappointing daughter to them for getting drunk while underage. Despite the fact that Cory and I rolled up drunk in that house more than a handful of times."

"I can't believe Cory told you that," I said, shaking my head. "It wasn't one of my more glorious moments."

"He thought it was hilarious."

"Did you?"

"Well, I think you renaming a thirty-year-old bird after knowing it two minutes was pretty funny. But, no, Cal. I actually thought it was sad."

"Sad?" I repeated, pushing up on his chest to look down at him, brows drawn together.

His hand raised, brushing my hair behind my ear. "It just wasn't you. You weren't the house party and getting drunk girl. I knew the only reason you would end up in that situation was because you were feeling shitty and decided to do something you never did- jumped over the cliff, blindly following the rest of the lemmings."

I tried to shrug it off, but shook off that urge and gave him the truth. "I was lonely," I admitted. "All my life, I had you and Cory to tag after, even when I knew it ticked you guys off. But then you both went away to college and I realized just how alone and isolated I was. So, eventually, I decided to try to go out and do normal teenager things. I went to sports games. I went to school dances. And then I went to that party. That was the last time I tried, though," I said, remembering the massive hangover I had, suffering through a power walk my mother dragged me on, not saying anything about my drunkenness, but punishing me for it the way only a mother could.

"You were never meant to blend into the crowd, Cal. That was the most amazing thing about you. You were your own person. And, for the most part, were that way unapologetically. That was why people like Amy picked on you. They didn't understand that. They were intimidated by it. So they tried to tear you down."

I swallowed hard against the lump in my throat at even thinking about asking what I was about to. "Did you and Amy ever..."

His loud, booming laugh stopped me mid-sentence, his body jumping under mine, making mine do so as well, his gaze on the ceiling for a long minute. "Honey, maybe I've been hard up in the past," he said, still grinning as he looked at me, "but I have never been that hard up."

"She was sort of all over you," I said with a shrug, not wanting to seem like I was jealous.

"Amy is not used to rejection so she doesn't take it well. Besides, while you and Cory might have been in the dark that I saw you as something other than a little-sister-type annoyance, I didn't fool Amy. She knew and she wanted to, I don't know, prove that she was better than you."

"She's really gonna hate me now, huh?" I asked, smiling a little. "I got the dream guy."

His smile went a little wicked then. "You had dreams about me, huh? How many of them were dirty?" My cheeks heated and he smiled wider. "In fact, how much do you want to bet there is a battery-operated device in this nightstand that you named after me?" he asked, moving to roll and go reach toward the nightstand.

"No!" I shrieked, trying to grab his hand. But he was faster. The drawer slid open, he reached in, and sure enough, he came back out with a baby blue vibrator I bought online several years back. It had served me well through the dry spells. His smile was victorious as he raised a brow at me. "Admit you thought about me while you pressed this up to your pussy on some lonely nights."

"Adam..." I said, cheeks on fire.

"Admit it, baby. I'll admit that it was you I thought about more times than I care to admit while I jerked off."

"Oh my God, stop," I demanded, rolling off to my side and covering my burning cheeks in my hands.

"Really, Cal?" he asked, his hand stroking down my bare skin on my side. "I've tasted you. I've been inside you. And you're still embarrassed to admit you touched yourself while thinking about me?"

He had a point. But that didn't mean I had to face him when I admitted it. "Okay, I thought about you."

"Hmm," he said and I heard the unmistakable buzzing of the vibrator turning on, my body stiffening in response. "Well, now I get to be the one doing the touching," he said, voice low, deep, promising.

And then he did the touching.

And I reaped the benefits of it.

Three times over.

Callie

"I'll start on the bookshelf," Adam called to me as he moved to grab a box that we had taped together that morning.

I looked up from the tea I was fixing, watching his strong, perfect body move across my small living room in a pair of thick charcoal gray sweatpants and a rumpled white tee, his hair messy. It was messy because my hands had gotten all tangled in it when I woke up to him kissing down my belly then going down on me.

It was a hell of a way to say good morning.

And after, he gave me slow and sweet before getting up and running out to grab bagels and a coffee for himself seeing as I didn't keep any in my apartment.

It wasn't that I was miraculously unafraid.

He didn't have a magic healing dick that took away all my trepidation and insecurity.

But he had sat up with me late into the night, talking. I talked about college, as did he. We discussed my family, his friends, his work. We talked about stupid, daily nonsense.

And the thing was... it was like no time had passed.

You'd have thought we had spoken every day for the past six years, instead of not seeing each other at all.

It was effortless.

We fell right back into old habits.

And, fact of the matter was, he was right. We had grown up together. We already knew all the good and bad and ugly and ridiculous about each other. While there were things we still had to learn, things that had changed, that had changed *about* us with time, we were both still the same people for the most part.

So while I was nervous as was possible to be about completely uprooting my life, of going back home, of starting a new job, about navigating a new relationship, I knew I had a strong support system. Even if things went completely to hell, I would have my mother and father and brother for support. That was a kind of comfort I hadn't known since I was a teenager.

I was taking a chance.

But it was time.

I had always played it so safe. I had been smart. I did everything by the book.

But it was someone else's book.

It was time for me to write my own.

"This one is weird. Who names a book *2006*?" he asked, moving to flip it open.

My heart stopped beating right then and there.

Because it wasn't a book; it was a journal. It was *my* journal from when I was fourteen. From when I first really understood my feelings for Adam. Coincidentally, it was also the same year that I learned how to give myself an orgasm. And there was maybe some detail about some of the fantasies I had had about him while doing so.

"Oh, is this..." he started, flipping open the first

page.

"No!" I shrieked, flying, positively *flying* across the small space of my living room, my sock-clad feet making me slide fully into his body as I reached for the journal. "No. Stop. This isn't funny. Give me it."

"Give me it, huh?" he asked, smiling wickedly as he pulled the book out of my reach. "I like the sound of that. You'll be saying that later."

"Adam, please give me that back. That's private."

"Come on, I just want to see if I am in there."

"You are," I confirmed, jumping and grabbing the book, using every bit of strength in my body to rip it from him.

"Did you draw our names in arrow hearts?" he asked, clearly amused, but I was narrowly avoiding a genuine heart attack over the whole thing.

"Yes, I did. And, no, I'm not going to show you."

"What else is in there? Did you write poetry about me?"

Okay. I had tried. I was going through an E. E. Cummings phase and I had tried my hand at it. It had turned out almost hilariously bad.

"*Yes*," I said, cheeks flaming.

"What did you compare my eyes to?" he asked, enjoying himself way too much.

Emeralds.

It was emeralds.

Never mind that his eyes were light green.

"You know... I used to love *The Diary of Anne Frank*. Now if she knew that school children were reading her personal words about her vagina, I bet she would have been completely beside herself embarrassed."

"Alright, alright," he said, shaking his head, reaching for me. "I was just teasing you, Cal. I wouldn't read your childhood journal. Though I would pay good money to hear that poem. Did it rhyme?" he asked, pulling me against his chest.

"Badly," I admitted, shaking my head at myself as I put my arms around him, dropping the journal into the box in the process.

"You totally did a *Risky Business* slide trying to get that journal away from me."

"That book has some very long, gushing pages about you in it."

"Gushing?" he asked, brow raising.

"I was fourteen. Fourteen-year-olds are notoriously long-winded and dramatic. Besides, I was in love. And fourteen-year-old girls in love..." I said, trailing off with a hand wave.

"Ten years," he said, shaking his head. "Got a lot of time to make up for," he added, his arm releasing my hip and his hand sliding between us.

"We already did some catching up this morning," I said, knowing we were never going to get any packing done at this rate and he only had a couple days off work.

"That wasn't catching up. That was present-day sex. And by my account, we have... let's see. You were legal six years ago. Let's say we average once a day, which, well, is conservative. Six times three-hundred and sixty-five is..."

"Two-thousand, one-hundred and ninety."

"Show off," he said, digging his fingers into my hip and making me let out a small squeal. "But, yeah, we have a lot of work ahead of us. And I, for one, would like to get started," he said, ducking his head so his lips met my neck as he pressed my hips into his, making his hardness push into my belly.

So then we got to catching up, that day taking the number down to two-thousand, one-hundred and eighty-seven.

Adam- 1 month

She refused to spend the first night at my house, claiming with wide eyes that her parents would know exactly why she was there. I smiled at that, at the fact that, having moved away young and stayed away, she had never had to go through the awkward phase of every adult when their parents knew they were having sex with a partner.

We moved all her stuff into her old room and the living space then we all went out to dinner, Cory included. After which she had given me a very brotherly *hug* goodnight in the parking lot that even her mother couldn't help shaking her head at.

And, well, I wasn't letting her get away with that.

I grabbed her arm as she turned to walk away, pulling her back toward me as one of my hands went behind her head just a second before my lips crushed down on hers.

I kissed her until she swayed completely against me, pulling back to see her hazy eyes and her swollen lips. "That's how you say goodnight to me, Pip."

The next night, her mother had encouraged her to come over to my place, claiming they were having company who would likely be staying late, then telling her to pack a small overnight bag.

Which she did, I imagined blushing the whole time.

I grabbed her cup of tea and my coffee off the counter and moved through the house. The house that she had already pinned a ton of design ideas for. "You know, I mean... if you needed any help. They're just, um, some ideas that are historically accurate."

She wasn't aware, but saying things like that showed me she was a mix of hopeful about a future with me, but nervous about my seriousness about it.

She had no idea how serious I was about her.

If I hadn't already been sure about her when I shoved a load of moving boxes into my car and drove down to D.C., I sure as hell was certain when I saw her again. When I watched her realize I had feelings for her too, when she saw how easily we clicked, even after all the years.

"Tea?" I asked, walking into the library which, it went without saying, was her favorite room.

She was in the chaise with an oatmeal-colored blanket she had brought over with her one night for just this purpose, always running just a little cold. Albus was underneath the chaise, swatting at the edge of the blanket with his little black paws. Her hair was piled on top of her head, a few tendrils loose around her face. She had yoga pants and a long-sleeve *Harry Potter* tee on.

I liked that too.

She didn't do that shit that some women did when things were new. She didn't wake up early to put on makeup so I thought she looked like a Photoshopped model first thing in the morning. She didn't dress up and always make sure her panties matched her bra.

No. She was the Callie I always knew, just in a different location.

And I found I really liked that.

I liked that she knew she didn't have to change for me.

She held up a hand in the air, eyes still completely focused on the book open on her leg, making it clear she had no intention in engaging me in conversation.

I handed her the tea and smiled, turning to move back into the hall.

My eyes fell on the shelf, as they always did.

It started with one book.

She always had a book on her and when she finished it, she had put it on my shelf, likely her lifelong dream of having a library making her do it. Then two days later, another book joined it. And then another. Then suddenly, R2-D2 was there too.

The shelf was full.

And I knew she would just continue onto another. She was settling in. Some of her clothes were in my closet. Her nerdy tea mugs were in my cabinet, as was a giant supply of tea and agave. There was a supply of potato chips in the pantry. But, aside from the day before her interview at the publishing house, she hadn't needed to reach for them.

Whether she realized it or not, she was slowly but surely moving in. And I was okay with not pushing the issue. It would happen eventually.

I loved her all my life.

And I had to wait twenty-four years for her to be mine.

I could be patient for a couple more months to have her stuff all over the house.

Callie- 1 year

We were sitting at the dining room table, everyone too full to move. Thanksgiving was even better when I wasn't stressing about my job or having to fly in, or worrying about seeing Adam again and that I might make a fool of myself in front of him.

I made a fool of myself in front of him daily, every day for about a year.

Every. Darn. Day.

But that was just how it was. I was clumsy and nerdy and tended to ramble about strange topics. Luckily for me, he found it charming. *The freak.*

I couldn't say I ever got used to having him. Every day felt fresh and exciting and borderline unbelievable. I had the man of my dreams, the guy I had loved since I was a kid still.

And he loved me back.

There wasn't a better feeling in the world than loving someone with everything inside you and knowing they loved you in return.

So much had changed in a year.

I wasn't in a job I hated anymore. In fact, I woke up in the morning excited to go because I knew there was a never-ending supply of amazing, undiscovered gems that I got to read, give the author thoughts on, then watch as it went to print and made another person's dreams come true.

I wasn't living alone in an apartment in a city I didn't particularly care for with no boyfriend and no family and no real close friends either.

I was in my hometown, living in my absolute dream house with my dream man, a short car ride from my entire family, with a whole group of bookwormy friends I had met through work.

Life was, well, it was perfect.

"Honey," my mom said, snapping me out of my daydream, "can you hand me that wine glass?" she asked, her eyes bright and active, though I had no clue why.

I turned away, grabbed the glass to the side of me, then went to turn back when I heard a clinking noise, looking down and seeing something inside the glass.

"What is..." I started, looking closer and seeing a ring.

I thought it was my mom's and tipped the cup to let it fall into my hand.

It was right about then that I realized Adam was

no longer on the seat next to me.

No, he was kneeling on the ground beside me.

My lips slid apart as I looked back at the ring.

His hand reached out, taking the ring from me and pulling my hand out to slide it on my ring finger.

"I love you, Pip. I always have. I always will," his voice was deep with feeling and I felt my heart swell in my chest, my eyes getting just a little bit misty at realizing I was going to marry the love of my life. "Even if you compared my eyes to emeralds," he added, making me let out a snorting laugh, swatting at my eyes.

For his birthday, after months of nagging, I had copied down and given him the poem from my journal. He had accepted it and had the grace to not tease me about it. For... all of a day. Then I never heard the end of it.

"Marry me," he half-demanded, half-asked.

"Alright fine," I said, sniffling slightly. "But just so you know, I am marrying you for the library," I said with a smile that he returned.

"I love you, Pip."

"I love you too."

XX

144

If you liked this book, check out these other series and titles in the NAVESINK BANK UNIVERSE:

The Navesink Bank Henchmen MC
Reign

Cash

Wolf

Repo

Duke

Renny

Lazarus

Pagan

Cyrus

Edison

Reeve

Sugar

The Fall of V

Adler

Roderick

Virgin

Roan

Camden

West

Colson

Henchmen MC Next Gen
Niro

Malcolm

Fallon

Rowe

Cary

Valen

Dezi

Voss

Seth

The Savages

Monster

Killer

Savior

Mallick Brothers

For A Good Time, Call

Shane

Ryan

Mark

Eli

Charlie & Helen: Back to the Beginning

Investigators

367 Days

14 Weeks

4 Months

432 Hours

Dark
Dark Mysteries
Dark Secrets
Dark Horse

Professionals
The Fixer
The Ghost
The Messenger
The General
The Babysitter
The Middle Man
The Negotiator
The Client
The Cleaner
The Executioner

Rivers Brothers
Lift You Up
Lock You Down
Pull You In

Grassi Family
The Woman at the Docks
The Women in the Scope
The Woman in the Wrong Place

The Woman from the Past
The Woman in Harm's Way

Golden Glades Henchmen MC
Huck
Che
McCoy
Remy
Seeley
Donovan
Cato

Shady Valley Henchmen MC
Judge
Crow
Slash
Sway

STANDALONES WITHIN NAVESINK BANK:
Vigilante
Grudge Match
The Rise of Ferryn
Counterfeit Love
Of Snakes and Men

OTHER SERIES AND STANDALONES:

Stars Landing

What The Heart Needs
What The Heart Wants
What The Heart Finds
What The Heart Knows
The Stars Landing Deviant
What The Heart Learns

Surrogate
The Sex Surrogate
Dr. Chase Hudson

The Green Series
Into the Green
Escape from the Green

Seven Sins MC
The Sacrifice
The Healer
The Thrall
The Demonslayer
The Professor

Costa Family
The Woman in the Trunk
The Woman in the Back Room
The Woman with the Scar
The Woman on the Exam Table

The Woman with the Flowers
The Woman with the Secret

DEBT
Dissent
Stuffed: A Thanksgiving Romance
Unwrapped
Peace, Love, & Macarons
A Navesink Bank Christmas
Don't Come
Fix It Up
N.Y.E.
faire l'amour
Revenge
There Better Be Pie
Ugly Sweater Weather
I Like Being Watched
The Woman with the Ring
Love and Other Nightmares
Love in the Time of Zombies
Primal

Under the pen name JGALA:
The Heir Apparent
The Winter Queen

Jessica Gadziala is the USA TODAY Bestselling author of over 100 steamy romance novels featuring all sorts of twisty and turny plots, strong heroines, lovable side characters, steam, and epic HEAs.

She lives in New Jersey with her parrots, dogs, rabbits, chickens, ducks, and her bearded dragon named Ravioli.

Made in the USA
Middletown, DE
18 November 2023